Moonlight on the Bay

A Katama Bay Series

Katie Winters

Chapter One

It was August in Savannah, Georgia, a sweltering, sweaty month that slowed the entire city to a near-stop. Aria Baldwin, a senior at the Savannah College of Art and Design, sat beneath a ponderous oak with a sketchbook open on her lap, as, above her, the limbs of the tree wound through the thick air, draped with moss. All morning, she'd dreamt of sketching out the first ideas for her senior year blueprints, hoping to secure a top grade and her dream job after this year's architecture classes. But her pencil remained dull in her hand, her thoughts hazy.

"There she is." A figure appeared on the other side of the moss, peering through the shadows to find her. Aria's stomach twisted. She hadn't wanted to be found.

"Benjamin," she said with a sigh. "How did you find me?"

Benjamin breezed through the moss happily and bounced to the ground beside her, wearing his very expensive Crest smile. His polo shirt, which had no sweat patches despite the humidity, spoke of his rich parents, lavish life, and his haircut, flouncy, like a show pony's, was his only way of living outside of his parents' desires for his appearance and his future. Surely after graduation, Benjamin would cut it.

"You're always here," Ben said. "Always deep in thought under this tree."

Ben pressed his face through the air between them and kissed her on the lips. She kept her eyes half-open, feeling dull and somewhere far outside of herself. When the kiss broke, Ben continued to smile at her like a lobotomized zoo animal.

"I can't stay long," Aria explained. "I have a meeting with Professor Heskew."

"Always running off to Heskew," Ben said.

Aria raised her shoulder. "I told you, he's the only one who gets what I'm trying to do."

"Right. Because the other people in the program just can't understand you," Ben said, half-sarcastically.

It was true that Aria often felt like an outsider within the architecture program. However, this wasn't such a hard situation for her to swallow, as she'd felt like an outsider since she was a girl. She was the youngest child of Kenny and Bethany Baldwin, a couple of Texan socialites with more money than they knew what to do with and two children (not including Aria) who upheld the Baldwins' mission in the world. When Aria had said she wanted to attend architecture school, her father had flipped his lid and demanded, *"Don't you know that as a Baldwin, there are duties you must uphold and attend to?"* Aria hadn't fully understood what he'd meant but had decided she would do everything on her own anyway, taking out loans and getting herself to Savannah. Her mother hadn't said a word.

"I have to go," Aria said, snapping her sketchbook closed. She stood, annoyed at Ben and his constant attempts to be in her orbit, to be near. In truth, he was also a link to her parents, the son of her father's business associate and someone Kenny Baldwin had professed to "loving like a son." When Ben had asked Aria to marry him in July, Aria had stuttered and spat with nerves, genuinely unsure about her allegiances. The "yes" she'd gotten out had sounded like a dying bird.

"I was just texting with your father about the sailing trip," Ben said, walking alongside Aria, toward the architecture school. "It's wild that we're both going to get out of an entire month of classes to travel around the Caribbean."

"What Kenny Baldwin wants, he gets," Aria said softly, quivering with fear at the idea of spending twenty-eight days on a sailboat with Kenny, Bethany, her sister, Natalie, her brother, Gregory, their spouses, and, of course, her nephew, Roger. Partially, her father had wanted to arrange the trip to celebrate Ben and Aria's engagement, which thrilled Ben and destroyed Aria's psyche.

Aria stopped outside the architecture building and gave Ben a hard look.

"What?" Ben asked, never once abandoning that smile.

"I just want to make sure you know something," Aria replied.

"Yeah?"

Aria swallowed. "I'm going to work as an architect. I fought hard to come to this school, to work alongside Professor Heskew, and to become the kind of artist I can respect. My father has always imagined I'll marry someone like you, settle down in Texas, and I don't know... plan charity functions and parties the way my mother does. But it just isn't going to happen like that."

Ben frowned nervously. He'd sensed that Aria had just described not only her mother's life, but also his mother's.

"I know you have big dreams, Aria," Ben said softly, with love in his eyes. "We'll make it work."

Aria said goodbye to Ben and walked up the steps of the main architectural building. When she reached the second floor of the old building, with its regal paintings and its ornate brickwork, she remembered with a funny flip in her stomach that she didn't have a meeting with Professor Heskew— that she'd made up the lie so she could get out of talking with Ben.

Why had she agreed to marry him again? Did a part of her still want to please her father, even after all he'd done? It was pathetic.

Aria sat on a cushioned maroon couch in the dark shadow of the old building, sketching in her book and dreaming about the next semester. Although she'd agreed to go on this sailing expedition, against her better judgment, she still hoped it would be an invigorating time of creativity, with the potential to unlock the blueprints she needed for graduation. She'd felt blocked lately, as though everything she drew was basic and boring.

To Aria's surprise, her phone pinged with a text from her mother.

MOM: Hi, honey! How is Savannah?

Aria raised both of her eyebrows. For years, her mother had seemed to exist as a puppet for her father's use, which meant that this text message was probably a gateway to Bethany and Kenny demanding something of Aria.

> ARIA: It's fine? What's up?

> MOM: I know you said you have a lot of work to do before we leave for our sailing adventure. Just wanted to check-in. :)

> ARIA: Um. Yeah. Maybe the sailing trip will even be helpful.

> MOM: Your father and I are looking forward to it. You know, we like Ben, and we can't wait to have him in the family.

Aria rolled her eyes and shoved her phone back into her pocket. Outside the window, a very soft breeze shimmered through the moss along the trees. As she sat, she tried to convince herself to walk back to her apartment, make herself a pitcher of very cold lemonade, and brainstorm. But before she could stand up, she heard footsteps down the hallway, followed by the gritty, deep, and rather wonderful voice of Professor Judah Heskew— her favorite teacher.

"Is that Aria?"

Aria turned and smiled up at him. As she did, she realized it was the first natural smile she'd given anyone in quite a while— perhaps since the last time she'd seen him. He was in his early fifties, with dark gray hair that curled around his ears, big honest eyes, and a thick beard that he often said was a prerequisite to being a professor. "*I promise, Aria. They demand it of you the minute you graduate with a Ph.D.*"

"Hi, Professor." Aria stood. "Pretty cold out, isn't it?"

Judah laughed. "Are you hiding out in here?"

"Something like that." Aria waved her sketchbook. "I'm brainstorming for next year."

"Your final year," Judah said. "I hope you're not too nervous. I know sometimes seniors can get in their own way."

Aria shrugged. "I always get in my way."

Judah chuckled again and beckoned for her to follow him. "Don't tell anyone, but I keep a secret stash of ice cream here in the building."

Judah's office was comfortable and airy, with big windows opening onto the park between historical buildings. Aria sat with a store-bought chocolate-chip ice cream cone and licked it languidly as Judah nibbled at an ice cream sandwich.

"I always feel like a kid when I eat these," Aria said. "And I always end up with a ton of chocolate on my face."

"That's part of the experience."

Aria nodded, eyeing the art along Judah's walls. For years, Judah had worked as a professional architect, and photographs of his rooms and buildings hung to show off his tremendous intellect and artistry. Once, Aria had asked Judah why he wanted to be a professor so badly, and he'd responded, *"It's hard to work with other people. Sometimes, you'll agree with the wife on something the husband undermines because it's too expensive. People accuse you of trying to rob them when you're just trying to make art."* Judah had followed this up by saying that Aria shouldn't think of this now— that, after graduation, her career as an architect could go several different directions.

"But being a professor works well for me. I'm grateful I made this choice," he'd finished.

For an hour or maybe two, Aria and Judah ate one ice cream and then another and chatted about their summers, architecture, and the next semester. Judah seemed unbothered by Aria's decision to go on a sailing expedition with her family, including *"that young man you're engaged to,"* which he always said with a knowing smile.

"Judah? Do you like being married?" Aria asked this absently, her eyes toward the window.

Judah pulled several strands of hair behind his ear and considered her question. "A great peace comes over you when you decide to settle down with someone. But it has to be with the right person."

"And your wife is the right person?"

Judah looked pained for a moment. "I don't know if anyone can honestly answer that question."

Aria's stomach flipped over.

"Are you asking this because you don't know if Ben is the right guy for you?" Judah asked, tilting his head.

"I don't know. I wish someone could just tell me if it was the right thing to do," Aria breathed.

"Why did you say yes?"

"I guess I thought I could still be an architect and a woman after my own heart while still maintaining some kind of relationship with my family," Aria explained, her cheeks becoming warm. "I know how much they love Ben. I know how much they want me to be a 'proper Baldwin.'"

Judah leaned back in his chair. "I'm surprised you still feel like that."

"Me too," Aria admitted. "I feel sort of ashamed about it."

"It's only natural to want to uphold some kind of love toward your family, even when you don't agree with them. But you cannot marry someone to appease your parents. It's a lifelong commitment." He leaned across his desk, his eyes fiery. "When you applied to this school, you did it without telling anyone what you were doing, without asking permission. And it sounds like you're asking my permission to break up with this boy. Don't do that, Aria. Don't belittle your emotions like that."

Not long afterward, Aria left Judah's office with renewed confidence and walked sullenly down the hallway, knowing it was nearly time to do what her soul demanded of her— to call it off with Ben. But as she passed by one of the libraries in the old building, she heard a number of people speaking, their laughter echoing. She paused, listening intently as someone she realized was her co-student, Julia, said, "I don't know what you thought of Aria's final project last semester, but it looked like a mess to me."

"Idealistic baloney," a student named Nate coughed.

"Professor Heskew just adores her," Julia said. "She can get away with doing anything."

"She could draw a blueprint for a shoebox, and he'd be like, 'Wow. That is so inventive, Aria,'" Nate said sarcastically.

"It's pathetic. She'll never make it in the real world," Julia continued.

Aria's throat felt thick, almost ready to completely close. Quickly, she turned on her heel and raced through the heat of the afternoon and down the steps. When she burst out of the architecture building, she hurried for her tree, where she wanted to find solace and think. But when she reached it, there was a couple beneath it, wrapped in one another's arms, uninterested in Aria or her sorrows.

As Aria returned to her apartment, overwhelmed with heat and over-sugared from the ice cream, she considered what Julia and Nate had said, along with Professor Judah Heskew's advice. The truth of it was she only had one love— and that was architecture. *But what if she was terrible at it? What if her parents hadn't wanted her to attend architecture school because she had no talent? What if she didn't belong there at all?*

One thing she knew for sure was that she had no love for Ben. Beyond anything, she had to remain true to heart, otherwise, everything would be lost.

Chapter Two

It was October in Grenada, an island in the Caribbean, and the sailboat that Aria's entire family had been sailing had just been destroyed and nearly sunk into the ocean.

Aria stood in stunned silence behind the rest of her family as her father, Kenny Baldwin, ripped a hotel concierge to shreds, demanding five of their best rooms, even this late into the night. "It isn't my problem that it's three in the morning. We've been through hell and back. We almost drowned."

Beside her father, Aria's mother, Bethany, glanced back and locked her gaze with Aria's. Aria wanted to plead with her mother to make her father stop, to tell him that ridiculing those in the service industry wouldn't get them to their rooms any faster. But after what had just happened out on the black water, as their sailboat had careened into an enormous rock, Aria just didn't have the energy.

"This is ridiculous," Natalie, Aria's older sister,

muttered to her husband, Malcolm. Malcolm placed his hand on Natalie's lower back and kissed her gently on the ear.

Gregory, Aria's older brother, carried five-year-old Roger in his arms as Roger slept soundly, his cheek a bulge against his father's shoulder. Aria's heart lifted at the sight. Because Roger was still so young and still willing to be silly and curious, Roger was perhaps Aria's favorite of all the Baldwins. Someday, Aria knew, Roger would become like his father and grandfather— stern, money-driven, and sure of himself.

As Kenny continued to bark at the hotel concierge to work faster, Natalie turned and touched Aria's arm. "Are you feeling all right?"

Aria stuttered, surprised at the question. For a moment, she'd forgotten that she was amongst her family at all, as though she sat in front of a television and watched them. "Yes, I'm okay."

"Whitney looked insane," Natalie muttered under her breath. "Dad sounds like he's going to sue the pants off her. Do you think maybe we shouldn't have gone with a female sailor?"

Aria's eyes widened in shock. "How is that your first thought?"

Natalie shrugged. "Aria, I'm just asking questions."

"Here's a hint. Maybe your questions shouldn't be overtly sexist?" Aria shot back.

At this, Natalie's face became frigid with anger. Under her breath, she said, "Why did you have to flirt with that sailor boy? You knew you were going to make Dad angry. Why do you always have to stir the pot?"

Aria gritted her teeth and muttered, "I never should

have come on this stupid sailing trip. This was the biggest mistake of my life."

Still, Natalie was partially right. When Aria had first spotted that handsome skipper, Cole, onboard the sailboat they'd planned to take for their twenty-eight-day adventures, she'd felt her soul catch on fire. There was something about him, about the honesty of his eyes, his sculpted muscles, his gorgeous tan. He'd made her laugh more in the past few days than Ben had throughout their relationship. Her parents were saddened that she'd ended her engagement with Ben, so much so that her mother had taken her aside to ask if there was any way Aria could consider getting back together with him. She knew Cole wasn't exactly the type of man Kenny Baldwin would have paired with his daughter. Cole had no plans to become a lawyer, to spend his days on the golf course, or to schmooze at parties for governor candidates. Cole's world was the open water. And Aria found herself doubled over with jealousy about it.

Aria was given a single room with a view of the water, which she awoke to the next morning. Sullen, she stood out on the balcony and watched the sunlight glitter across the waves and the tourists take their stance on the sands, ready to bask the day away. *Where was Whitney? Where was Cole? How bad had the damage to the boat been?*

Over the next several days, Aria's family carved out a small "family vacation" for themselves on the island of Grenada, most of which Kenny Baldwin spent in a state of perpetual complaining. "I can't believe what that incompetent sailor did to us," he said, usually speaking of Whitney. "Both of them were probably inexperienced in this type of trip or boat," he added, speaking, now, of both Cole and Whitney.

Aria spent most of her time away from her family, wandering the beaches with her sketchbook and thinking again about architecture school. Ever since she'd heard the other students ridiculing her work in the architecture building, she'd felt completely at a loss, as though every bit of her creativity had officially dried up. The first few weeks of school, prior to her departure for the sailing trip, had left her moody and inarticulate. She'd even avoided Professor Heskew, frightened that he was wrong about her talent. Besides, she didn't want the other students to think he gave her preferential treatment just because they ate ice cream together and talked about whatever was on their minds.

To Aria, Professor Heskew was one of the first real friends she'd had in Savannah, and not being able to see him during that time had nearly destroyed her.

A few days after the sailboat accident, Aria ran into Cole on the boardwalk in front of their hotel. He looked upset and lost and told her that he planned to return to Martha's Vineyard, his home. He insinuated that he never should have left. Aria's heart cracked at the edges, imagining this handsome man at home with his family, with his mother who loved him. The way Cole spoke about Martha's Vineyard was poetic, filled with nostalgia. She'd never felt so romantic about where she'd come from. It made her ache to see it for herself, if only to see the world through Cole's eyes. She'd begun to think that her own life fell short.

Aria sat on the beach, her pencil poised over her sketchbook and her mind awash with frantic thoughts. Suddenly, the sand shifted to her left, and she turned to find her mother, Bethany, coming toward her in a cream-colored dress, her hair shifting lightly in the breeze. Last

Aria had heard, her mother and father had gone for massages that morning and hadn't planned to meet with their children until evening.

"Can I sit down?" Bethany asked Aria, tilting her head.

Aria swallowed and closed her sketchpad. "Okay."

Bethany sat and eyed the sketchbook. She looked as though she wanted to see what Aria had drawn, and Aria prayed she wouldn't ask, as it was little more than a few random lines.

"I guess you're getting ready to return to Savannah," Bethany said.

"Yep," Aria replied, her voice hard, although she hadn't even bothered to look at flights yet. The money she had left from loans and such could hardly get her back, let alone pay for her rent for the rest of the year. When she returned, she would have to hustle to find a job anywhere or grovel for her father's cash.

"Your father is so angry," Bethany said softly, rubbing her cheeks.

"He's always angry about something," Aria muttered.

Bethany sighed. Aria sensed she knew Aria was right but wasn't willing to say it. "He contacted his lawyer this morning to get the ball rolling on suing Whitney."

Aria bristled and glared at her mother. "There's so much Dad doesn't understand about Whitney." Aria felt protective over the woman on the boat, a woman who'd lived her life with such freedom.

Bethany frowned. "What do you mean?"

"I was researching her the other day, and you know, her dad died the day of the accident. I mean, how would you have felt if you'd learned someone you loved died when you were out on the water?"

Bethany's eyes glowed with compassion. "I don't think that will change your father's mind."

"It should," Aria shot back. She then wiped her hands on her thighs and jumped up, scanning the horizon. "Is he around?"

"He's at the hotel bar," Bethany said sadly. "But don't go to him, now. He's in a mood."

"So am I." Aria walked across the sand, back toward the hotel, where she entered the lobby and walked toward her father. When she got right up behind him, she cleared her throat and said, "I have a proposition for you."

Kenny's back was very stiff. After a moment, he turned and met Aria's gaze, looking at her like a businessman looked at a client rather than a father at a daughter. "Yes?"

Aria sat on a stool two away from him and knocked on the counter to order a gin and tonic. Kenny stayed with his beer.

"I don't want you to sue Whitney," Aria said.

"Why do you think you have any say in that?"

"I know that I don't. But I'm willing to make a trade," Aria said.

"Go on."

"I will never ask you for money again," Aria said. "We can put it in writing, and I'll be, well, not even your daughter."

Kenny's eyes shimmered.

"That's worth a lot to you," Aria said. "You won't have to worry about me anymore. I'll just be— elsewhere. And I'll never call you for help. I'll never ask you to put cash in my account. I won't be a privileged Baldwin anymore. I'll just be..." She shrugged and dropped her chin, wondering who she would be after all this. "And let's be honest. It's not like you've ever thought of me as one of your own, anyway."

Kenny sucked in his cheeks, clearly enraged. "All I can do is think about it."

Aria turned and locked eyes with him. "I need your word, right now, that you won't sue Whitney. That you won't make that woman's life a living hell." She raised her hand to shake his, and slowly, he slid his hand into hers and lifted it up and down. At this moment, Aria felt older and wiser than she ever had. Finally, it seemed she was up to figuring out who she was and what she wanted.

But that night, as she packed her suitcase and poised at her computer to purchase a flight, she found herself routing a ticket to Boston rather than Savannah. The trip to the Caribbean had changed her, as had her breakup with her fiancé and her understanding that the other architecture students in Savannah didn't respect her work. She needed a break, a time of introspection— she needed to breathe some cold and clean air.

There was no telling what Cole Steel would think upon her arrival. There was nothing that told her he even liked her as a friend, save for those big, honest eyes that seemed to pierce all the way through her. Unlike any man she'd met in Savannah or in all of Texas, Cole Steel was the kind of guy she wanted to fall deeply in love with and make it last an eternity. If Cole wasn't her future, she needed him to help her understand how the world worked. She needed him to take her out onto the open waters between Martha's Vineyard and Nantucket and let her scream to the sky above. Never, in all her life, had she felt good enough, right enough, smart enough, or pretty enough— not to be a Baldwin, anyway. And if she was going to be in the midst of a horrific identity crisis, she needed to do it where nobody knew her name, except for Cole.

Chapter Three

Carmella could hardly believe her luck. In her mid-forties, she'd given birth to her first child, a gorgeous girl named Georgia, and for a little while at least, fallen into idealistic motherly bliss. She slept when the baby slept, nursed as she watched the snow fall outside, and laughed herself silly with her husband, Cody, about the joys of their life together.

But now that it was January and Georgia was a few months old, something had changed. The main thing, of course, was that Georgia no longer liked to sleep. She cried all through the night, the morning, and the afternoon— her little face all scrunched up and her feet kicking exuberantly. It broke Carmella's heart to hear her daughter scream like this. She did everything she could to calm her down, read every single baby blog, talked to her sister, Elsa, and even called a sleeping specialist. Everyone told her that this was probably just a phase, one that Carmella wouldn't remember later on.

It had gotten so bad that she and Cody had begun to trade off sleep schedules to ensure that neither of them entered a state of psychosis. This led Carmella to miss Cody so much, to miss the warmth of his body beside hers at night, and she often cried when Georgia cried now, laughing to herself as she said, "Cry when the baby cries! Sleep when the baby sleeps!" There were so many "sayings" in motherhood, all of which made her feel like she wasn't doing a great job.

It was mid-January, the middle of the afternoon, when the doorbell rang. A rarity, Georgia was asleep in the next room, and Carmella walked to the door to find her older sister, Elsa, smiling at her. Carmella fell forward and hugged her sister like she was the last person on earth.

"I'm sure I look exhausted," Carmella said as she led Elsa inside to pour them both cups of tea. "It's been a really hard time. Harder than I thought!"

Elsa winced. "You sit. I'll make the tea."

Carmella was too tired to argue. She collapsed at the kitchen table and watched as Elsa made herself at home in the house she and Cody now shared. It had always seemed easy for Elsa to make a home for herself, to have that maternal instinct and to have authority over situations. This had never been Carmella's thing. Just as the water began to boil, the doorbell rang an additional time, and Elsa turned and said, "I'll get it!"

Carmella waited in stunned silence as Elsa led a young woman Carmella had never seen before into her kitchen. She was blonde and very pretty, wearing ripped jeans and a big sweatshirt that said something about sailing on it.

"Carmella, I want to introduce you to Aria," Elsa said.

"Hi," Aria said sweetly, extending her hand so Carmella could shake it.

Carmella said hello, feeling confused.

"You need a break," Elsa announced. "You've been trapped in this house for far too long with little Georgia."

Carmella's heart shattered at the thought of taking a few minutes away from her daughter. Then again, part of her knew Elsa was right, that if she didn't make time for her own needs, she would fall apart.

"Aria is going to babysit," Elsa explained. "She's been babysitting for others around the island and comes highly recommended. Not to mention, she's Cole's friend."

"How do you know Cole?" Carmella asked.

"It's a long story," Aria said with a wave of her hand. "We met in the Caribbean."

"Oh!" Carmella smiled, remembering that Cole had raced competitively and worked as a sailing instructor in the Caribbean before returning home in the late autumn. "Is it a good story?"

"We can catch up with Aria another time," Elsa urged. "Why don't we hit the road now? We can have tea at the Lodge after we've had our massages."

Carmella groaned at the thought of a massage. Her back and shoulders ached from lack of sleep, from cradling Georgia, and probably, just from aging. "All right. All right. But I stink! I haven't showered in—"

"Don't worry about it," Elsa said. "We can take nice baths at the Lodge, too. The very best suite is empty today."

"You spoil me," Carmella said, then glanced back at Aria, who seemed to be twenty-four or twenty-five, her eyes bright. *Could she trust her with Georgia? Was this right?*

"She'll be fine," Elsa assured her as she tugged Carmella through the front room. "Bye, Aria! You have my number if you need anything."

"That's right," Aria called back. "Have a great time!"

At the Lodge, Carmella and Elsa slid into side-by-side baths filled with plenty of suds, the air simmering with lavender and other calming oils. Carmella closed her eyes and felt her thoughts quiet, floating away from her through the wonderful air.

"So," Carmella said, her eyes half-open. "Is Aria Cole's girlfriend?"

"I don't know," Elsa answered. "He doesn't tell me anything."

"How did you meet her?"

"I stopped by the bar a week or two ago, and they were both up there," Elsa explained. "She was working behind the counter, and he was drinking a beer after a lesson."

"She looks like she comes from money. Doesn't she?" Carmella suggested.

"I got that vibe," Elsa affirmed. "But then, I found out she's been living in one of those tiny and broken-down apartments on the outskirts of Edgartown?"

Carmella's eyes opened wider. "Wow."

"Cole mentioned something about her stepping away from her family for a while," Elsa explained. "At any rate, she and Cole seem thick as thieves, whatever they are to each other."

"I hope they're in love," Carmella said wistfully.

"You're the poster child for the best friends-to-lovers story," Elsa teased.

"Georgia is our miracle baby," Carmella said. "I love

her so much that I sometimes think my heart will break. But she's driving us insane!"

Elsa laughed. "Kids do that. You think it's bad now, then just wait until she's in her teens."

"You should have warned me," Carmella joked.

"I'm pretty sure all of pop culture already warned you," Elsa said.

After their baths, Carmella and Elsa donned soft white robes and slippers and walked downstairs for their massages. There, two young women who'd just begun to work at the Lodge that winter since Carmella's absence massaged them with powerful hands, ones that didn't seem to belong to their slight frames. Carmella lost herself in the feeling of her muscles loosening, the kinks falling away.

"Would you have ever followed a boy to Martha's Vineyard?" Elsa asked thoughtfully, midway through the massage.

Carmella's eyes opened part-ways. She knew her sister was still thinking about Aria. "You mean, if I'd met him in the Caribbean?"

"I guess."

"I don't know. Probably not, but not because I didn't want to," Carmella said. "I lived so far from my feelings for so long, and I guess that's how I was able to watch Cody marry and have a baby with someone else." Carmella shivered at the memories, during which she'd cried at home alone at night, even as she'd told herself how happy she was for Cody.

"I just hope Aria didn't abandon something else that was important to her," Elsa said. "No matter how much power women have in this new generation, it's still easy to doubt ourselves, our powers, and make mistakes."

"Do you honestly think Cole would be a mistake for Aria?"

Elsa laughed gently. "I think anyone can be a mistake to the wrong person. Even my wonderful son."

After massages, Carmella and Elsa went to the beautiful eating area of the Lodge, with its floor-to-ceiling windows that featured a gorgeous view of Katama Bay. It was a chilly yet gorgeous winter day, one wherein the sun shone brightly through the frigid branches of the surrounding trees. Carmella and Elsa feasted on the nutritious food the Lodge had to offer. Salads with walnuts, goat cheese, dried cranberries, a ginger carrot soup, and a beautiful slab of pink salmon seemed to open Carmella's eyes wider than they'd been since her baby was born.

"I have a gift for you," Elsa said, leaning over her steaming soup with a mysterious expression on her face.

"Oh? Is it the ultimate tip to get my baby to sleep? Because I think I'm on tip forty-five with no luck."

Elsa laughed gently and squeezed Carmella's wrist over the table. "Unfortunately, I'm not a miracle worker." She dropped down to fish a dark brown book from her ledger, which she placed between their bowls of soup.

Carmella lifted the old leather book, which seemed in every way a journal, somebody's long-past record of time. When she opened the first page, she read aloud: "The Diary of Tina Remington." A shiver raced up Carmella's spine. "My gosh. Where did you find this?"

Elsa's eyes shimmered with excitement. "I had a few boxes at the old house hidden in a closet somewhere. They were filled with Mom's journals and photo albums. I thought this one, in particular, would be of interest to you because..." She trailed off, her smile widening. "Well, it's the journal Mom kept when she was pregnant with you and then for about a year after you were born."

Carmella's jaw dropped. For a moment, she stared at her sister, genuinely shocked. She wanted to protest, at first, to remind Elsa that their mother hadn't loved Carmella in the slightest, that, after their brother Colton's death at a young age, Tina had hardly looked at Carmella in the eyes.

"Carmella," Elsa said sternly, as though she could read her mind, "You know all that love you're feeling for Georgia right now? That huge, insurmountable, powerful love?"

Carmella nodded dumbly.

"Mom felt that for you, too," Elsa continued.

"Have you read the journal?"

"I read the first couple of pages," Elsa said. "Just to make sure it was the right time period. An early entry talks about the names she and Dad were considering for you. One of them is Hildy. Can you imagine if your name was Hildy?"

Carmella flipped two pages in to find the list, then burst into laughter. "I dodged a bullet there."

"You really did," Elsa said.

As Elsa drove Carmella back home, she pressed the journal against her chest, terrified and very pleased to have this fresh window into her mother's life. Throughout the early weeks of Georgia's life, Carmella had been overwhelmed with thoughts of Tina, about what she had been thinking immediately after Carmella's birth, and about the bond she'd surely built with Carmella during those early days. It was bizarre never to speak to her mother about the strange yet beautiful moments of early motherhood. Now, it was like Tina could whisper through time and space and share everything that had been on her mind.

"I wish you would have had her journals when you were a young mother," Carmella said as Elsa braked the car in Carmella's driveway.

Elsa waved her hand. "I had Dad. He was such a help back then, telling me stories about when I was a baby and how young and foolish he and Mom felt at the time."

Carmella's heart lifted slightly. She'd always felt that their father, Neal, had loved Elsa much more than he'd loved Carmella. This was something she supposed she would never get over, even so many years after Neal's death.

"Thank you for a beautiful day," Carmella said, draping herself through Elsa's car to hug her tightly.

"Tell Aria I'm out front," Elsa said. "I can drive her wherever she needs to go."

"Will do." Carmella got out and walked to her front door, her ears craning for the sounds of her baby's cries. But when she opened the door, she found Georgia asleep in her bassinet in the living room, with Aria sound asleep on the couch. The young woman had her arms crossed over her chest and her head flat across the couch cushions, and Georgia looked adorable and pink-faced, her little hands in fists.

Carmella clipped the door closed behind her, which made Aria jump up with surprise.

"I'm sorry to wake you!" Carmella whispered, smiling at Aria.

Aria shook her head. "Don't worry! Did you have a good time?"

"It was so wonderful." Carmella leaned over the

bassinet and smiled at her baby, whom she'd missed so much. "Was she okay?"

"She was great!" Aria explained as she gathered her coat and her shoes. "A few cries occasionally, but mostly, she just kept sleeping. She also seems to be a big fan of my singing, which makes her the only person in the world."

Carmella's eyes widened. "You must be a baby whisperer."

"Oh, gosh. No way. Georgia made it easy on me." Aria pulled on her winter hat and shrugged.

Carmella hunted through her wallet for cash, paying a bit more than she would have since the girl lived in those horrendous apartments on the outskirts of town. "Elsa says she'll drive you wherever you need to go."

"I'm off to my other job!" Aria said with a laugh. "There's no end to the grind, is there?"

Carmella winced as she watched the young woman stride back into the cold and hurry into Elsa's car. In the front seat, she strung the seatbelt over her chest and chatted easily as Elsa smiled and backed the vehicle into the road. When they disappeared down the street, Carmella returned to the couch and dropped against it, where she leafed through her backpack to find her mother's journal again.

Although she knew Elsa had given the journal as a sweet and easy gift, Carmella had begun to fear it. Being a new mother meant experiencing dark and strange emotions, ones that were not easy to explain to other people. *What if Tina's dislike for Carmella had actually begun when Carmella was two or three months old? What if Colton's death hadn't had anything to do with it? Maybe this diary was better left unread.* Carmella stood and slipped the book into a nondescript place between other books on her shelf, praying that, at some point, all that sleep deprivation would make her forget about it. And just as she turned away from the shelf, Georgia's eyes opened, and she let out a howling scream. It was show time.

Chapter Four

It was early February. Aria awoke in the single bed she'd purchased second-hand for very little and stretched her legs and arms, staring out the window at yet another very cold day in Martha's Vineyard. Around her was the rinky-dink apartment she'd managed to get for herself not long after her spontaneous arrival to the Vineyard last October, when she'd abandoned her family, architecture, and everything she'd ever known to pursue a quest to "find herself." But this deep into being poor and lonely, she wasn't often sure she remembered why she'd done any of it.

Aria made herself a pot of coffee and checked her messages, of which there were three. One was from her mother, who frequently checked in to see how Aria was doing.

MOM: Hi, honey. How are you doing up there in the cold? Your father and I were talking about visiting New York City in the spring. Maybe you would like to meet us

there? I know things are difficult between you and your father, and the sailing incident didn't help. But couldn't you find it in your heart to forgive him— especially since he hasn't gone after Whitney Silverton, just as he promised you? I love you so much, Aria. And I sometimes don't know what to do with the fact that I haven't seen you since autumn. Mom.

Aria blinked back tears and considered how to respond to her mother, a woman who could write such pretty things but never stand up to Kenny Baldwin, a man who seemed made of ice.

There were two other messages, one from her advisor at the Savannah College of Art and Design, asking her how she wanted to proceed. Although she'd dropped out last semester, she only had a few more credits till graduation. "It seems like a waste, doesn't it, not to proceed with graduation? Especially after how hard you've worked." Aria immediately deleted the email, feeling dead inside.

The final email was from none other than Professor Judah Heskew, who'd written her several times since he'd learned of her abandonment of her coursework. Some way or another, he'd found out about the sailing accident, and sometime around Christmas, he'd asked Aria if the accident had had something to do with her dropping out. Aria had written back to say that she just wasn't sure about her future anymore and that she wasn't sure she had "it," whatever it was that made someone successful.

Now, Judah wrote:

Hey, Aria. I just wanted to check in and let

you know that I will be hosting an online class for the second half of this semester regarding the architecture of Frank Lloyd Wright. I remember you once told me you 'weren't quite sure about the guy,' and I was hoping you could enter the class and give your opinions on that. Perhaps those credits could be helpful to you when you decide to return to school and officially graduate. As I've said many times, I find your work incendiary, and I hope to help you hone it and work your way into the architecture world.

Aria's nose shivered at the email, but she didn't delete it. Instead, she threw her phone back onto her bed and stood in her cold kitchen and sipped her coffee. When she again looked at the clock, she realized it was just about time for her to shower, get dressed, and head off to the bar, where she had to work from three to midnight— a killer shift that often made her enough money to pay a week's worth of rent.

Since Aria had begun working as a part-time babysitter for Carmella and a full-time waitress at the bar, she'd managed to save up enough money to purchase a clunky little Chevy, which worked just enough to get her most places she needed to go. Sometimes, at the stoplight, it stalled out on her, and she had to turn the key and listen to it sputter and sputter until it finally turned over again. To Cole, she had said this was "the most exciting moment of my day." Cole had laughed and called her crazy, just as he always did.

Aria hurried around the establishment, setting up chairs and wiping tables as the music blared in the speakers. Cole was teaching a few lessons that afternoon but had said he would be around the bar around six or seven to drink a beer and say hello, which Aria couldn't wait for.

It was true that Aria saw Cole just about every day. They met for coffee, a beer, or a walk along the freezing beach, making one another laugh until they had to run inside and warm up. Aria understood how strange it had been for Cole when Aria had followed him to Martha's Vineyard in October— that it had bordered on insane territory for him. But for some reason, he'd always been there for her, driving her to the grocery store when she ran out of food, helping her secure this job at the bar, and even holding her when she cried of loneliness.

For some reason, Aria hadn't told Cole the extent of why she'd left everything behind. She hadn't explained that she'd lost her creative spirit, that the other people in her architecture program thought she was a hack, and that although she didn't want to be anything like her parents, she also wasn't sure she wanted to be anything like herself, either.

A mix of gruff, happy, and red-cheeked sailors entered the bar around four, ordering drinks and laughing with Aria. Aria found it easy to pretend to be joyful, to crack jokes. Often, she could even convince herself that she was just fine, cleaning pint glasses and pouring more.

"I saw that handsome man of yours out on the docks earlier," one of the older sailors said to her as she breezed past.

"I don't have a man, Johnny," Aria said to him, to which he howled.

"If that Cole kid doesn't lock you down, he'll regret it for the rest of his days," Johnny said.

Aria rolled her eyes privately and turned back toward

the bar, shame stewing in her gut. In truth, how Cole looked at her made her feel like the only woman in the world, as though the world had been created so that she and Cole could fall in love. But they'd hardly touched one another since her arrival in October. Sometimes, when they hugged, Aria felt as though her body was on fire.

Cole entered the bar around six-thirty, all smiles and filled with stories. He sat at the bar as Aria filled his pint glass and told her about his adventures that morning, the wild chaos of the seas, and how he wasn't sure why he'd ever tried his luck in the Caribbean when it was so obvious to him now that the Atlantic was his only home, just as it had been for his father, who'd passed away.

As Cole spoke, another couple of patrons sidled up at the bar next to him and ordered beers, then asked Cole a few questions about his day.

"Where are you from?" Cole asked one of the sailors, his pint lifted.

"Just sailed up from Savannah," one of them explained with a southern drawl.

"You're kidding!" Aria smiled excitedly as Cole and the two other sailors gaped at her.

"Have you been to Savannah?" Cole asked her.

"Um." Aria's head swam about what she wanted to share and how she wanted to share it. "I lived there for a few years."

"No way," one of the sailors said. "What part?"

"I was going to the Savannah College of Art and Design," Aria explained, flipping her hair nervously.

Cole's eyes flickered with intrigue. "You never told me that."

"A woman doesn't have to share everything about herself," one of the Savannah sailors told Cole with a laugh. "Tell us, honey. What was your specialty? You look like a painter to me."

"Or a sculptor," the other said.

Aria rolled her eyes at their fake flirtation. "I was studying to become an architect."

Cole's lips parted with genuine shock. "An architect?"

"That's a crazy impressive field," one of the sailors said.

"Did you drop out?" the other asked.

"Just last semester," Aria said. "I'm really close to graduating, but I don't know if I'll go through with it. I found this new career, you know. Tending bar."

Cole continued to look at her as though he'd never seen her before. Avoiding his eyes, she refilled their pint glasses and chatted to the guys about Savannah, about what she missed in that beautiful city.

"To be honest with you, I needed a break," she explained. "My life felt like it had been flipped upside down."

"That isn't Savannah's fault," one of the guys said.

"I know. It's a me-problem," Arai affirmed.

He didn't always, but on this night, Cole stayed till close and helped Aria clean up, wiping tables and even mopping the floor. Afterward, he palmed the back of his neck and said, "Are you hungry?" And Aria's heart flipped over at his sincerity, his desire to spend just a few more minutes together.

They decided to grab a couple of pizzas and meet back at her place, where they could watch some trash television and chat without being overheard by anyone they hardly knew. They ordered at the cheap place that didn't charge for extra cheese, then drove through the black and cold night to Aria's shoddy apartment, where they dug into the pizzas and sat at the edge of her bed. Cole's lips glistened with the grease from the pizza, and Aria stirred with longing. She'd never in her life been more eager to kiss someone, and it seemed to her that as time passed on their friendship, her window of opportunity was narrowing.

This deep into friendship, they could only ever be friends. That was the science of it all.

"I can't believe you never told me you were studying to become an architect," Cole said, his eyes like blue daggers.

Aria set down her pizza and cleaned her hands with a napkin. "It's not really a big deal."

"It is," Cole insisted.

"I was supposed to go back to Savannah after the sailing trip," Aria explained. "But I just couldn't. I felt so off. So unsure of myself."

Cole furrowed his brow. "Was it because of the accident?"

"No. I mean, I don't know." Aria could still remember the jagged fear of that night, how she'd been so sure that she and her entire family were about to drown in the inky depths.

"An experience like that changes a person," Cole muttered. "It's part of why I returned to the Vineyard."

Aria nodded. It took her every bit of strength not to reach over and touch his hand. But now, as though he sensed how much she wanted him, Cole inched away from her and crossed his arms over his chest. The refusal of her love seemed apparent. Aria stood and walked angrily toward her kitchen counter, wanting to scream at Cole, to demand why he spent all this time with her but didn't love her.

As she stalled at the counter, she parsed through her mail, most of which were bills, save for one envelope with her name and address. There was no return address. She frowned at the calligraphy of her name, which was in handwriting she didn't recognize. Cryptic.

"I just don't think you should give up on your dreams," Cole continued as he stood to clean up the pizza and put the leftovers away. "I mean, you went to that Savannah art school for a reason, didn't you?"

Aria blinked up at him, regretting ever telling him about it.

"What's that?" Cole asked, gesturing toward the envelope in her hand.

"Oh. I don't know. Just a bill or something," Aria lied, shoving it under the pile of mail. She smiled at him nervously, suddenly so exhausted that she thought she might collapse. "I'll see you tomorrow, yeah?"

Cole nodded, his cheek twitching. Again, there was a strange energy between them, something Aria felt she couldn't penetrate. It always seemed there was so much left unsaid between them.

"Sleep well," Cole said as he zipped up his coat and tugged his winter hat over his head. Then, he disappeared into the black night and left Aria stirring in confusion, her brain foggy from too much cheese. Already, the strange envelope on the counter was more or less forgotten, and she stewed in sorrow and loneliness until she finally fell into the release of sleep.

Chapter Five

It was mid-March, and Carmella was at the gym, of all places. In the mirror, she watched herself on the treadmill, walking with her Kindle up on the platform, her legs striding easily, with more muscle and strength than they'd had in quite some time. Ever since Aria had proven herself to be a "baby whisperer," Carmella had opted for much more time out of the house, using Aria's talents about three times a week to carve out space for herself. It seemed that now, Carmella was able to think clearer, sleep deeper when she had time, and love Georgia, Cody, and Gretchen, when Gretchen was around, with greater depth and responsibility. As a single person, she'd never cared so much about herself, but now, she understood that caring for herself was a necessary element in caring for everyone else.

When Carmella drove home, she found Aria in the kitchen with baby Georgia in her arms, singing to her as Georgia cooed gently and happily.

"Aren't you a perfect sight?" Carmella laughed as she entered to take Georgia into her arms.

Aria blushed and then joined Carmella's laughter. "I didn't hear you come in!"

"I'm glad. I've never heard your singing voice before. It's something special."

"It's not. I just practice in the car all the time," Aria explained.

Carmella remembered Aria's clunky Chevy out front, which she'd just purchased about six weeks ago. The car had belonged to a friend of a friend of Carmella's, and Carmella had been able to make the connection, which had ensured that Aria had gotten a very good deal.

"Why don't you stay for tea?" Carmella suggested as Georgia fell asleep in her arms. "Unless you have to run back to the bar?"

Aria agreed and placed the kettle on the stovetop, whistling to herself as Carmella went to the next room to put Georgia in her crib. After the water boiled, they brought their tea into the living room and sat on the couch calmly as a sharp late-winter, early-spring draft burst against the house outside.

"This winter must have been hard on you," Carmella suggested, "being a southern girl and all."

Aria wrinkled her nose and sipped her tea. "There were a lot of reasons this winter was difficult. I wouldn't say the weather was in the top five."

This wasn't the first time Carmella had seen something of herself in Aria, that same lost, aimless twenty-something she'd been twenty years ago.

"Have you considered visiting your family at all?" Carmella asked.

Aria shook her head. "We're not close."

"I wasn't close with my family, either. For many years," Carmella said.

Aria's eyes widened with surprise. "Really? But you and Elsa seem like best friends."

"That's a pretty new thing. If you had told me a few years ago that I would be married with a baby, and best friends with my sister, Elsa, I would have said you're crazy." Carmella stalled, then added, "Oh, gosh. I sound like an old lady telling you, 'Life changes when you least expect it!' Ignore me."

"Don't worry. I've seen enough movies to know that's supposed to happen," Aria joked. "It's just hard to imagine it will happen to me."

Aria's eyes drifted around the room, then paused at the bookshelf near the couch. Recently, Carmella had pulled out her mother's journal again, burning with curiosity, but she'd only read the first two or three passages before returning them to the shelf.

"That little brown book looks like it's filled with ancient secrets." Aria pointed to it.

Carmella laughed. "Something like that. It's my mother's journal from when she was pregnant with me and right after I was born."

"Wow. How is it?"

"I can't really bring myself to read it," Carmella said softly. "My mother was a difficult person in my life for many years. When I was a child, my family was out horseback riding, and I made a huge mistake— something I could never take back. My brother died because of it, and I don't think my mother ever forgave me. A few years later, she died in a horrible car accident."

"My gosh." Aria's face was slack with sorrow.

"Anyway, I felt like such an outsider after that," Carmella finished, trying to raise her tone of voice. She felt strange speaking about the horrors of her past so close to where Georgia slept in her crib.

"I don't blame you," Aria breathed. "My mother is... well. She's a difficult woman. I feel like she's trapped in a terrible marriage with my money-obsessed father, and she's just too obsessed with money herself to ever get out of it. But she did tell me, a few years ago, that after I was born, her depression was so bad that she had to be hospitalized for a little while."

Carmella's lips parted with surprise. "I'm so sorry to hear that."

"She only told me once and said it in a way that let me know I wasn't supposed to bring it up again. But I often think about her sitting in a hospital, too upset to be my mother." Aria stuttered, then tried to smile. "I don't think I've ever told anyone that before. It's one of those deeply ingrained family memories that aren't supposed to see the light of day."

"Every family has those," Carmella assured her.

"I know that, in theory. The thing is, I'm trying so hard not to be a member of the Baldwin family anymore, so it's strange that I carry these memories around."

Carmella bit her lower lip, unsure if she should say what was on her mind. "Do you ever hear from your mother?"

"Sometimes."

"I'm sure she misses you so much," Carmella said.

Aria shrugged, her eyes glinting with tears that she refused to let fall. Carmella knew she was too strong to cry in front of Carmella, who was, to Aria, still a stranger.

"I really wish that I could talk to my mother again," Carmella said suddenly, "if only to ask her some questions about the past. To ask her if she really disliked me that much or if it was just a story I created in my head." Carmella stuttered, then said, "I just can't imagine your mother doesn't love you to pieces, Aria. You're a brilliant young woman with so much to offer the world. I don't know if enough people have told you that before."

Aria was quiet for a long time, and Carmella was sure she'd overstepped. Still, as Aria gathered her things and eventually said goodbye, taking Carmella's payment with her, she thanked her with a very soft voice, which made Carmella hope she'd gotten through to her.

Not long after Aria left for the afternoon, Cody's car appeared in the driveway. He smiled as he drove, his hands at ten-and-two, then parked in the garage and entered through the door in the kitchen. Although she was still in her gym clothes, Carmella rushed toward him and threw her arms around him. "You're home early!"

Cody laughed and kissed her, his eyes alight. "I thought I'd come see my girls. And..." Cody removed his backpack off his shoulders and shook it, "I bought some supplies to cook tonight. I figured we could eat something besides frozen pizza for a change. What do you say?"

"Why are you spoiling me like this?" Carmella said, grabbing his backpack and searching through it to find ingredients for truffle pasta with fresh parmesan, one of her favorites.

"Do I have to have a reason?" Cody kissed her again, then took her hands and danced with her through the kitchen as she cackled.

"Remember when we used to do this as middle schoolers?" Carmella said.

"I remember that you refused to dance with me when you thought other people were looking."

"I was such a moody teen. I wish I could go back, shake her, and tell her to appreciate that wonderful skin."

Cody dropped her over his arm as though they were Fred Astaire and Ginger Rogers, and then he said, "I loved your moodiness. I was obsessed with you, remember?"

Suddenly, the baby monitor exploded with Georgia's cries, and Cody lifted Carmella and said, "I'm on it." He grabbed a bottle from the fridge, which Carmella had filled from pumped milk, and then set himself up on the couch with baby Georgia, who immediately calmed as he fed her. Carmella sat beside him, her head on the back cushion of the couch, thinking again about Aria, about what she'd said about her mother.

"I wish there was a way I could make sure Georgia knows how much I love her," Carmella said then.

"Where is this coming from?" Cody asked.

"I just feel that so much about love and relationships gets lost in translation. People are too frightened to say how they feel or what they actually mean."

Cody's eyes widened slightly. "I mean, we almost never got together."

"Case in point."

Cody adjusted Georgia tenderly in his arms. "I think it's all a matter of learning from our parents, right? You know what your mother did that hurt you, which means you can be conscious about the way you handle Georgia's adolescence?"

Carmella remained quiet, her eyes on the brown book on the bookshelf. She prayed that Cody was right, that she could find a way through the labyrinth of being a mother to Georgia and a stepmother to Gretchen, to show them love and kindness in everything she did.

But ultimately, what happened in the future was up to Georgia and Gretchen. They could turn out like Aria, running as fast and far away from home as possible. Her heart shattered at the thought.

After Georgia fell asleep, Cody returned to the kitchen to start the pasta. After she pumped, Carmella sipped a glass of Bordeaux and picked up her mother's journal, daring herself to read another few passages before dinner. In her mind, she called it "research" to ensure Georgia wouldn't see Carmella the way Carmella saw Tina. Generational trauma had to stop here.

November 17, 1977

I told Neal I can't do it. That I can't hack it, and maybe I was never meant to be a mother in the first place. He snorted at that and pointed to Elsa's bedroom down the hall, where she continued to sleep. He said I had better buck up and get on board with the motherhood thing since I already had a toddler and a second baby in my arms. I gazed down at Carmella, this gorgeous dark-haired creature I brought into this terrible world, and wept until Neal stormed upstairs and slammed the door.

It is truly such a shame to feel this way so soon after giving birth. I wallow around my house while Neal spends his days at the Lodge (that Lodge that takes up all his time!). Neal is able to tell himself continually how important he is. But my only importance to him and maybe even to me is to raise these girls.

November 19, 1977

I came off as cruel in my last entry.

I don't want to look back at these in a few years and remember myself as this spiteful, terrible woman. In truth, I want to look back and remember myself as this beautiful new mother, nursing my second daughter while my oldest plays at my feet. I want to make baby food for Elsa while Carmella sleeps in her crib, and I want to have dinner made on time for Neal when he returns home from a hard day of work.

But the reality just isn't that, at least not right now. A friend has told me that it's probable I've entered a state of depression in the wake of the birth. I don't know why we, as a culture, need to "label" everything. Maybe I'm just unhappy, and maybe that's okay.

Suddenly, Carmella heard her name from the kitchen and then slammed the journal closed.

"Carmella? Do you mind coming here quickly to see if the pasta is al dente enough? I never can tell," Cody said.

Carmella blinked tears from her eyes and placed the diary back on the shelf. When she walked toward Cody, her head spun with her mother's words. Even from the very beginning, when she'd been only a baby, Carmella's presence had destroyed her mother's psyche. Then again, the seventies had been a much different time. Mental health hadn't been understood in the same way, and women were often neglected, told to make the dinner, do the laundry, and keep their figure trim.

"Are you okay?" Cody's eyes swam in front of her, heavy with worry.

"Oh. I'm okay," Carmella said, not wanting to dig into her mother's past, not then. She kissed Cody with her eyes closed, giving thanks for such a remarkable, understanding, and helpful man, the only man she could ever have partnered with. "I'm just so glad you came home early."

"I'm going to try to do it more often," Cody said. "I hate that you're here by yourself so often. Taking care of a baby is not an easy feat. And we never set out to do this alone."

Chapter Six

The phone call came toward the end of April. Georgia was on her back in a sunbeam, her little legs and arms up in the air as she played with a toy that hung over her. Carmella was stretched out on the couch, exhausted yet blissfully happy, watching her daughter grow into her boisterous personality.

"Hi, Elsa!" Carmella said, smiling into the phone. "How are you on this gorgeous spring day?"

"Oh my goodness. You just won't believe this." Elsa sounded ecstatic. "I'm driving toward your house right this minute. I hope you're there?"

Carmella laughed and rose on the couch to watch Elsa turn onto her driveway and scurry out of the car. The minute she reached the top of the porch steps, Carmella opened the front door and put her hand on a hip. "What's gotten into you?"

Elsa looked wide-eyed and erratic. She hurried into the house and sat beside Georgia, her eyes alight as she gently pinched Georgia's foot.

"Elsa! What's going on?" Carmella demanded.

Finally, Elsa raised her gaze to Carmella and whispered, "They're both pregnant."

Carmella shook her head, not sure she understood. "Who?"

"Alyssa and Maggie," Elsa said.

"What?" Carmella was confused. She already knew that Alyssa had decided to carry her sister, Maggie's embryo, to term, as Maggie had struggled with IVF. But how could Maggie also be pregnant? "I thought Maggie and Rex were getting divorced?"

"They are," Elsa whispered. "This is another guy!"

Carmella's head spun. "Another guy? But Maggie and Alyssa just moved to the island!"

Elsa laughed and popped to her feet as Carmella made space for her on the couch, clearing away Georgia's clean laundry, which still needed to be folded. Meanwhile, Elsa explained what she knew about Maggie's new "surprise" man, that he was the son of Heidi, the woman who owned the bookstore called The Dog-Eared Corner. Incidentally, Maggie had just purchased the bookstore to ensure that Heidi could maintain control of it. Furthermore, Maggie and Alyssa had been instrumental in uniting Heidi and her son, David, who hadn't returned to the island in more than seven years. It was a doozy of a story, one that ended with Maggie's surprise pregnancy.

"So, it was Rex's fault," Carmella breathed, remembering all the horrific IVF treatments, Maggie's sleepless nights, and her fears that she would never be a mother.

"It seems like Rex has been dragging Maggie down in more ways than one all this time," Elsa affirmed.

Elsa went on to say that a big party was planned at the Remington House that weekend and that Carmella, Cody, Gretchen, and Georgia were invited.

"I won't live there much longer," Elsa added sadly, her face a mix of emotions. "Bruce and I will be able to move into our new place sometime this summer, which is hard to believe."

Carmella hugged her sister, closing her eyes with the joy she felt for Elsa— that she'd been able to go on and fall in love with a kind and wonderful man, even after Aiden's death. Carmella had watched from the sidelines for decades as Elsa and Aiden had married, had children, and gone through the textures of time together— her jealousy following her around like a shadow. But when Aiden and their father had passed away within the same year, Elsa had fallen apart.

With the building of her new life with Bruce, they'd sprung for a beautiful property just down the shoreline from the Remington House. There, they would live out the rest of their lives together.

That weekend, Carmella and Cody dropped Gretchen off at Cody's ex-wife's, waving exuberantly as Gretchen turned back on the top of the porch steps. Afterward, they drove themselves and baby Georgia to the Remington House, where spring sunlight shone brightly across the sands, the budding trees, and the windows that had been opened to bring in the glorious breeze. It had been a very long and oftentimes depressing winter, yet Carmella and everyone else were ready to open their arms to a springtime of change.

As Georgia slept, Cody took her upstairs to set up the baby monitor, leaving Carmella to find her sister, stepsister, Janine, and stepmother, Nancy, in the kitchen, preparing snacks and desserts for the party ahead. Janine, Alyssa and Maggie's mother, was excited, wearing a bright red dress and lipstick to match, her eyes dancing as she told a story. When Carmella entered, Janine sprung forward to hug Carmella, then said, "Can you believe it, Carmella? Both of my girls?"

Carmella laughed. "Where are you going to put all these babies, Janine?"

Janine blushed. "I don't have the first idea. I suppose we'll have to fill up this house."

"That's just fine with me," Nancy said, breezing past to open the fridge. "Carmella, would you like a glass of chardonnay?"

Carmella agreed to a single glass, then followed Elsa to the back porch, where Alyssa, Maggie, and Mallory sat with lemonade and cookies. Apparently, Mallory's son was with her ex-fiancé, but Lucy, the toddler Maggie and Alyssa were caring for in the wake of Alyssa's ex-boyfriend's stint in rehab, sat happily in her highchair, smacking her hands together.

"Hello, darlings!" Carmella bent to hug both Alyssa and Maggie first, followed by Elsa's daughter, Mallory.

"Hi!" The three of them greeted her in singsong voices and passed her a cookie.

"Mallory was just telling us about her recent case at the law firm," Maggie explained proudly.

"I don't think I could ever wrap my head around what you do," Alyssa said, leaning forward in her chair.

Mallory blushed. "All I do is study. That's the only reason I'm getting through."

Carmella sat beside Maggie and nibbled on her cookie, which Maggie had baked for the occasion. Just as with everything Maggie baked, it was to die for. It melted in her mouth decadently, the chocolate chips oozing.

"So, Maggie. Who is this David guy?" Carmella asked, smiling as Maggie's cheeks flashed crimson.

"She's in love," Alyssa teased.

"Oh, whatever," Maggie said, "David and I find ourselves in a pickle together, I guess." She placed her hand on her stomach, adding, "Neither of us ever thought we would leave New York City nor ever have our own children. Yet here we are, living in Martha's Vineyard, and..."

Carmella nodded, understanding that Maggie still didn't want to jinx the pregnancy by speaking of it too much, that she'd had too many miscarriages to know it wasn't for sure yet.

"I keep telling Maggie that we're both going to have twins," Alyssa joked. "And since both of these pregnancies are legally Maggie's, I'm out of here immediately afterward. Good luck with the quadruplets, Sis!"

"Don't forget Lucy," Maggie added, rolling her eyes at Alyssa's comedy. Carmella smiled, considering the weight of what these young women planned to do. It was true what Alyssa said, that both babies were legally Maggie's. *So, where did that leave Alyssa when the babies came? And where would Lucy fit into all of that? Did Hunter, Lucy's father, ever plan to return to pick Lucy up?* It was all so unclear.

Alyssa lowered her voice to ask, "I heard Cole's mistress has been helping you babysit?"

Carmella laughed. "I didn't know she was his mistress."

"I don't know anything," Alyssa said sadly. "I keep probing Cole for information, but he's impossible to crack."

"Turns out not everyone likes to gossip as much as we do," Maggie said.

"What's she like?" Alyssa asked Carmella.

"Aria? Oh, she's very sweet," Carmella said. "I think she's a little bit lost right now. I can't imagine it was easy to leave her entire family like that."

"It sounds like they were terrible people," Alyssa said.

"I don't think that makes it any easier," Carmella reasoned.

Alyssa grimaced. "It's so hard to get a hold of Cole these days because he's always with Aria. I just want them to fall in love and get it over already."

"And where's your love story, huh?" Maggie demanded.

Alyssa blushed and sipped her lemonade. "I'm pregnant, Maggie. Nobody is going to fall in love with me for a long, long time."

"I don't believe that for a second," Maggie said.

The hours at the Remington House drifted forward, punctuated with beautiful conversations, many laughs, glasses of lemonade, and scrumptious treats. When Carmella and Cody finally left that evening, they were both exhausted, ready to collapse in bed, at least until Georgia woke them up for a feeding around two-thirty.

"Your family is insane," Cody muttered as he rolled over in bed a little later, "in the very best way, I mean."

Carmella rubbed his shoulder, her heart tripling in size with love for him. She kissed his naked back gently, then heard Georgia coo and begin to weep with surprise. Suddenly very awake, Carmella tugged herself from bed and carried Georgia into the living room, where she calmed her back to sleep again.

Afterward, almost without thought, Carmella's eyes returned to the brown diary on the bookshelf, which she'd hardly picked up since she'd begun to read about her mother's very deep depression in the wake of Carmella's birth. She'd carried the knowledge of it around like a secret, tucked behind the rest of her thoughts. She wanted to be careful not to spill the beans on her mother's sorrow and her father's moods, especially not to Elsa, who loved their father so completely. What Elsa didn't know wouldn't hurt her.

Now, Carmella opened the diary once more, parsing through the events of that first winter with baby Carmella until she discovered something truly surprising.

January 18, 1978

Neal thinks I'm weak for going to therapy, but he doesn't say so out loud. I arranged for a babysitter so that I could leave around two-thirty, hours before Neal would ever be able to leave the Lodge, with the hopes that I could take an hour or two for myself immediately after the session. Neal would never have understood my need to be alone. He would have said it means I don't love my children— which is insanity! What kind of mother doesn't love her children? But what kind of mother can genuinely say she's happy every day, as the monotony of her children's lives makes her bones so tired and her thoughts wired with sorrow?

The babysitter arrived a few minutes early, which felt like a blessing, and I literally ran out the door like a madwoman. I hardly bothered with makeup and didn't even think about what I was wearing. I just wanted to be gone.

I'd heard the name of the therapist before. Dr. Oliver Matthews sounded to me like a man draped in prestige who'd gone to an Ivy League university and graduated top of his class. I imagined him to be in his sixties or seventies, with a thick beard and contemplative eyes.

I couldn't have been more wrong.

The man seated on the other side of his office from me was only a little bit older than me. He has brown eyes, shaggy reddish hair, and thick glasses that he frequently adjusts on his nose, as you imagine therapists do. And as we chatted at the beginning of the session, he looked at me, really looked at me the way I don't know anyone has. It reminded me that Neal had spent the previous few years of our marriage looking all the way through me like I was a ghost sent to earth to do his laundry.

Today was our very first session. I didn't tell Oliver much about myself besides the basic details. He asked me what I wanted to get out of the sessions together, and I wanted to laugh until I cried, but instead, I told him I'd just like a bit more clarity on my life. He said he can help me with that. Let's see if he can.

Now, I have to make dinner for my toddler and my husband and try to force all thoughts of Oliver Matthews from my mind. Oh goodness. What a handsome, kind man!

Over the next few diary entries, Tina Remington recounted her conversations with Dr. Oliver Matthews with tremendous detail. Within their conversations, Tina finally opened up about how lonely she felt in her marriage, how little she felt Neal cared for her, and how fearful she was that her low opinions of herself and her life would somehow infect her children. Oliver listened intently, made notes, and asked all the right questions. Oftentimes, Tina wept in front of him without embarrassment, pleased that he allowed her this beautiful time to feel at peace.

By the third or fourth week of her sessions with the therapist, Tina Remington found herself in another nightmare. As her happiness increased daily, her dissatisfaction with her husband intensified. More than that, she fell deeper in love with Oliver. She often fantasized about him all through the afternoon and evening, to a point where Neal hardly bothered with her anymore because she didn't listen to anything he had to say.

Once, Neal grabbed her arm as she left the room, and he glared at her and said, "Did you hear what I just asked you?" And Tina lifted on her toes and kissed him on the forehead as though he was a child. "I'll pour you a scotch, honey," she heard herself say, although her mind was miles away, wherever it was Oliver Matthews lived. In many ways, she no longer lived with Neal, and she was no longer herself, either.

Chapter Seven

It was May, which meant that Aria had lived on Martha's Vineyard for seven months. Most of that she had spent in the deepest and darkest depression, during which she'd questioned every decision she'd ever made and every little thing about her personality. But now, as the sun warmed in the gorgeous blue sky above and as Aria opened her heart to the possibilities of the new season, she no longer thought so much about what she'd abandoned at Savannah College of Art and Design. She no longer dreamed of herself as an architect nor considered herself anything but a lost woman in the world who was doing what she could to pay the bills. She was also a woman very much in love with Cole Steel, but that was something she was too afraid to say aloud.

Aria was hard at work at the bar. It was a seventy-five-degree day, and tourists had already arrived on the island in droves, sailing across the Sound and finishing their days with pints at the bar. Aria kept one eye continually on the door, watching for Cole, who'd promised to drop by immediately after he took a group of six tourists out for a sail. Aria had joked, *"Isn't that how we met?"* But Cole wasn't willing to joke about that time of their lives, nor about Whitney Silverton, and he'd scrunched his nose and said, "I'll see you around seven."

Just as he'd promised, Cole Steel entered the bar a few minutes after seven. He was tanned with blonde hair highlighted from the sun, and he flashed her a confident smile as he swaggered forward. Aria's heart burst in her chest. *Had she ever felt like this about anyone?* She thought of Benjamin, her ex-fiancé, that maybe had she loved Benjamin half as much as she loved Cole, she might have convinced herself to marry him.

"How's it going, Aria?" Cole sat on his usual stool as Aria poured him a pint.

"It's been crazy here," Aria said. "Non-stop tourists."

"And non-stop tips?" Aria's boss breezed behind her, carrying a keg of beer.

"It hasn't been bad," Aria affirmed, feeling the wad of cash in her server's apron. "How was it out on the water?"

Cole explained that the tourists hadn't been half-bad, that they'd asked lovely questions and even helped him with the boat as they'd come in. "I got a decent tip, as well," he added, beaming. "It's only spring, and I already have a hunch this will be a really good summer."

Aria's heart flipped over as she imagined long, beautiful sailing rides alongside Cole, who'd promised to teach her to get really good at sailing.

"I met up with Alyssa this morning," Cole went on, speaking of his cousin, who he was close with. "I don't remember if I've told you this, but her sister, Maggie, is pregnant, too! Isn't that crazy?"

Aria's jaw dropped. "Wait. I thought—"

"That Alyssa was carrying Maggie's baby? She sure is. It's wild, isn't it? So many babies in the family."

"I guess I could get more babysitting gigs," Aria joked.

"Plenty." Cole laughed. "Although I can't imagine Maggie will want to spend too much time away from her babies. She's already really fidgety if you take Lucy away from her for too long, and Lucy isn't even hers."

Suddenly at the door, a voice rang out. "Is that Whitney Silverton?"

As Cole turned quickly, Aria lifted her eyes to watch as the beautiful, world-famous sailor, Whitney Silverton, glided into the bar. As usual, she was long-limbed and slender, with long, vibrant hair that spoke of treks across the great ocean. Like a woman in a film, she whipped off her sunglasses and smiled at Cole knowingly, her eyes alight. Aria remembered that while they'd been on the sailboat together in the Caribbean, she'd been so jealous of how chummy Whitney and Cole had been with one another, as though Whitney, who was quite a bit older than Cole, secretly wanted to date him. *Was Aria losing her mind? Or had Whitney come back to Martha's Vineyard to get Cole back?*

"Cole Steel, as I live and breathe!" Whitney hurried toward Cole and hugged him, overjoyed.

Cole laughed and hugged her back, genuinely glad to see her. Another guy at the bar ordered a pint of beer, and Aria burrowed herself behind the bar, trying to hide away.

"I want you to meet my boyfriend, Rowan," Whitney said, waving her hand toward a very handsome sailor type who walked across the bar. "I think you might have met him before at this very bar."

Cole laughed and shook Rowan's hand. "That night before you left! Of course!"

"She tracked me down," Rowan explained, glancing at Whitney with love in his eyes. "I never imagined the great Whitney Silverton would ever slow down enough to let someone else join her, but somehow, I made the cut. Of course, I always bring my A-game on the water just in case she decides to throw me off."

"Good idea," Cole said. "You sticking around for a while? Want to grab a few pints?"

Whitney and her new boyfriend, Rowan, sat at the bar next to Cole, exuding life and the salty air. Aria poured them each a pint and placed them on the counter, not making eye contact with Whitney, praying she wouldn't recognize her from the Caribbean trip. But after Whitney took a sip, she glanced up and spotted Aria, and her face transformed immediately.

"Wait a minute!" Whitney placed her beer back on the counter. "It's Aria, isn't it?"

Aria grimaced and eyed Whitney, unsure of what to say. Whitney then turned to stare at Cole, her jaw slack. "Wait a minute," she repeated. "Are you two together?"

Cole and Aria sputtered at once.

"No! No." Aria laughed.

"Not at all," Cole affirmed as he slid his fingers through his hair.

Aria felt as though a knife had gone all the way through her stomach.

"Aria, what the heck are you doing here?" Whitney asked, shaking her head. "I thought I'd never see any of the Baldwins again."

"She doesn't plan to see them, either," Cole explained.

Whitney nodded. "Your dad was a piece of work, wasn't he?"

Aria blushed and crossed her arms over her chest. "I couldn't be in that family anymore. The trip to the Caribbean proved that to me."

"I'm sorry you had to go through that," Whitney said honestly. "And I'm glad you found a home here in Martha's Vineyard. I think my brief time here last autumn really changed my life. And if you've spent time with Cole's family, I imagine you've felt great love."

Aria nodded. "One of his aunts has been really lovely. I babysit her daughter."

Suddenly, another group of sailors entered the bar, and Aria was forced to work pouring beers, making cocktails, and hurrying around the bar as the noise increased. Someone played Queen on the jukebox, and someone tried to perform with the same register as Freddy Mercury but failed. Aria tried to get herself into the chaos of the bar, to feel the beautiful energy, but always, she had one eye on Cole, who spoke excitedly to Rowan and Whitney about all things sailing.

In truth, Aria knew that one day, Cole would find a girlfriend who would whisk him away on an adventure. And Aria would be left on Martha's Vineyard, wondering why on earth she'd followed her heart on a whim like that. What a silly girl she was!

Around nine that evening, a few young women from Edgartown entered the bar. They were beautiful, wearing layers of makeup, their skirts shorter than anything Aria had at home, and they slid up onto the stools alongside Cole and smiled at Aria as though she was much lesser than them. Aria supposed she was. After all, she was only a bartender at a dive bar.

Aria served the young women the drinks and then sped off for another table that needed her, keeping tabs on Cole. The woman who'd sat directly beside him had begun to chat with him, playing with the end of her skirt. Cole laughed at something she said, and Aria felt her soul momentarily leave her body.

When Aria returned behind the bar, she listened intently as the woman beside Cole told him all about her routine at the gym. To her horror, Cole asked her questions as though he was genuinely interested. Their conversation was so boring, lacked any intellect, and seemed worlds away from what Aria and Cole often spoke about. And yet, he seemed interested! What was going on? Had the world fallen off its axis?

"Aria!" Whitney's voice came through the chaos of Aria's mind, and she turned to stare at the most famous female sailor in the world, who was smiling as though she knew everything going on in her mind.

"Do you need another drink?" Aria asked.

Whitney smiled and nodded. "Two beers, please. And a moment of your time."

Aria wanted to roll her eyes but poured the beers instead, listening as the young woman beside Cole laughed at one of his jokes. Oh gosh. Aria had never seen Cole go home with anyone else or heard about any of his dates. But Aria had been on Martha's Vineyard for seven months, meaning he'd probably gone out with at least one or two girls. She was sure that number was higher.

"So, tell me." Whitney took her beer and raised it. "Why did you come to the Vineyard?"

Aria blushed and stepped away from Cole and the young woman. "It's beautiful here."

"There are plenty of beautiful places," Whitney said.

"This particular one has been cold for most of the time you've been here."

"I don't mind the cold," Aria lied.

Whitney leaned over the counter so that her lips were very close to Aria's ear. "Have you told him yet?"

Aria was frozen with fear. "What are you talking about?"

Whitney gave her a look that meant business. "Come on. I saw how you looked at Cole on that sailboat last autumn."

Aria was quiet, remembering how she'd fallen so quickly for the young and handsome sailor who'd seemed the direct opposite of everything she'd ever known.

"Aria, time is all we have, you know?" Whitney said, her smile waning. "And men can be a little bit dumb sometimes."

Aria wanted to tell Whitney her greatest fear —that Cole already knew Aria was in love with him but wasn't in love with her back. She'd imagined telling him so many times, but each time, in her daydreams, he said, *I just don't feel the same way.* And she'd fallen apart.

How could Aria explain to Whitney just how badly she'd messed up her life? She'd felt out of her mind when she'd dropped out of architecture school, but mostly she'd felt lost and confused when she'd stepped away from her family. Many months after, she finally felt on solid ground again. But if Cole told her he didn't love her back, she would be thrown back into the chaos of those dark thoughts that she fought hard to keep at bay. She couldn't chance it.

"I just can't," Aria said to Whitney as shame made her cheeks burn.

Whitney nodded as Cole burst into laughter at something the young woman said. "I'm in my forties, Aria," Whitney said timidly. "I wasted so much time on men who didn't care about me, who didn't have my best interests at heart. Cole isn't like them."

"I know that," Aria said stiffly. "But that doesn't mean he has to love me back." With that, she turned on a heel and hurried away from the bar, Cole's friend's laughter, and Whitney, who seemed to know so much about the ways of the world. In the bathroom, she gasped for air as the world spun around her.

Somehow, Aria was able to get through the night. Around midnight, the young women left the bar, with the flirty one giving Cole her number before she left. Whitney and Rowan said goodnight, explaining they planned to sleep in their sailboat. And Cole, who would have normally gone home with Aria to share a pizza, placed his baseball hat on his head and said goodnight. Aria's heart shattered in her chest.

"Good night!" Aria called as, one after another, everyone left the darkening bar. "See you later!"

Aria drove back to her dreary apartment with blurry, tear-filled eyes. She then stood at her kitchen counter with a glass of wine that she hardly drank, staring into the black night outside her window. For the millionth time, she read over a recent email Professor Judah Heskew had sent her. It explained the events on campus that semester and that he would still be interested in looking over any sketches she'd drawn over the past few months if she cared to share them.

Also, her mother had written her an email telling her about the events in the town she'd grown up in, along with how much she missed her. Aria felt so far away from both of them and so far away from herself.

As she cleaned her countertop, Aria stumbled into the envelope she'd received a few months ago, upon which someone had scrawled only her name and address and nothing else. In all the chaos of making money and falling in love with Cole, Aria had somehow forgotten it.

Now, Aria grabbed her key and slid it through the envelope, removing what looked to be a cut-out from an old and yellowed newspaper. *What the heck?*

Aria stared at the photograph for a long time. In it, several young women and men stood in a line at Savannah College of Arts and Sciences, all in graduation gowns, some of them laughing together and others staring into an unseen distance. Aria recognized the building behind them as the architecture building on the campus, and a stab of fear and intrigue entered her heart.

Beneath the photograph, the newspaper had listed the names of the Savannah College of Arts and Sciences architecture program graduates. The list was long, filled with names Aria would never know. But then, her eyes stopped on one that she would have recognized anywhere:

Bethany Quinn.

Aria's ears rang as she searched the crowd to find the young woman who could only be her mother. There she stood, between Billy Rodgers and Ginny Tyson, in a graduation cap and gown, her smile electric and filled with pride. In it, she couldn't have been more than twenty-one or twenty-two, and she held her diploma aloft as though it was the secret to the questions of the universe.

Aria collapsed on the edge of her bed and searched through the envelope for some sign of who had sent the photo. The handwriting on the envelope itself was not her mother's, which she would have recognized anywhere.

Filled with adrenaline, Aria searched on her phone for some sign of Bethany Quinn at the Savannah College of Arts and Sciences. Aria's mother was forty-nine, which meant that she would have graduated around 1995 — just before internet records. There was nothing online that suggested Bethany had ever been on Savannah's campus at all.

Aria dropped back onto her pillow, wracking her brain to remember what her mother had looked like when Aria announced she wanted to go to the Savannah College of Art and Design. *Had she looked joyful? Nostalgic? Had she said anything at all?* Throughout that journey and even after she'd moved, Aria had felt so alone, with no help at all from her parents. *Why had Bethany kept this information a secret?*

Aria began to write her mother an email, one that demanded answers. But halfway through, she closed her computer. Whoever had sent this photograph wasn't her mother. It was crystal clear that her mother didn't want her to know about her past. *What was she hiding?* And how could Aria get to the bottom of it without asking her mother the truth?

Chapter Eight

It was a balmy day in mid-May when Carmella dared to continue reading her mother's diary. She'd read it in bits and pieces throughout the past couple of weeks, watching her mother fall deeper in love with her therapist, Oliver Matthews, as she avoided her husband as much as she could. Each entry threatened to break Carmella's heart. Each spoke of a woman who was so lonely that the only person she felt understood her was the man she paid to listen to her talk.

But all that changed in April of 1978.

April 13, 1978

I've done something terrible. And yet, in my soul, I know it's the most magical thing I've ever experienced in my life.

I had a session with Oliver yesterday that I had been looking forward to all week, counting down the hours. It was the single thing getting me through Elsa's temper tantrums and Carmella's sickness. (It seems like they've both been sick all spring.)

Yesterday with Oliver, I broke down and told him I wasn't sure if I could do it anymore. I couldn't remain with my husband. I couldn't continue to think of myself as this boring, lifeless thing that was secondary in Neal's life. And at that moment, Oliver removed his glasses, stood, and sat next to me on the couch with his hand on my knee. He'd never touched me so delicately before— I mean, he'd hardly touched me at all. He asked if he could talk to me as a friend rather than as a therapist, and I was so nervous that I just nodded. I could not breathe.

He told me:

"I meet women in lonely marriages all the time. It's a frequent plague of our time. Normally, I do what I can to help these women heal. I help them patch together their marriages and their psyches. But with you? I struggle to know what to say because I find myself wondering why on earth you would stay with this man."

I nearly fainted when he said that. It was beyond my wildest dreams, honestly. I wanted to fall against his chest and cry as he held me. I wanted to tell him that I never should have married him. I wanted to ask him where he'd been in my life when I'd "needed" to get married.

And then, Oliver did something insane. He took out his business card and wrote down the name of the hotel, the number of the hotel room, a date, and a time. He said nothing else as he slid it into my palm.

Wordless, I stood up and walked from the office, feeling as though I was about to float into the sky. All evening and all night, I asked myself, should I really do it? Should I really see him? Yet I knew that I'd already made up my mind.

The babysitter came on time, thank goodness, and then

I walked away from the house, down the beach, then cut through several tourist houses to find this little hotel he'd picked. I know he picked it because the place is discrete. The people who own it are hush-hush about things like this, which is essential on such a small island.

I went to the hotel room Oliver had written on the card and knocked. I thought I was going to pass out with fear. Then, his voice called, "Come in," and I walked through to find him seated on the bed, wearing clothes he always wore, his eyes alight behind his glasses. When I looked at him then, I had this feeling that I was coming home for the first time in years. We fell into bed after that. It was no longer a time for words.

Carmella continued to read, through April, into May, and finally, June of 1978. Throughout, she could feel herself and Elsa within the pages, two little things who needed their mother so badly, even as their mother was preoccupied elsewhere.

June 11, 1978

Oliver asked me to come to New York City with him for a weekend trip. I knew it was outside of reason for me to ask Neal if I could go, but then, we had a stroke of luck. Neal was asked to go to a business conference in Iowa, of all places, and he planned to go. (Note: it's not like he asked me if he could. It was assumed that I would watch the girls.)

After I found out about Neal's trip, I asked the babysitter if she wanted to make a ton of cash. Her eyes lit up at that, as she's saving up to move to the city herself. I asked if she could watch the girls from Friday to Sunday, and she said that would be fine. Neal swims in cash and often doesn't know how much he spends, so I knew that I could manipulate the books without him seeing how much I'd given her.

Oh, goodness. The trip to New York was a dream. Right before I left, I removed my wedding ring and boarded the ferry to get off this stifling island. Oliver was waiting for me on the mainland in his convertible, his hair windswept, and I dropped into the passenger side as though I do it all the time. Up in that front seat, we kissed with reckless abandon, far away from the island, my husband, and my girls. I felt like someone else. I felt free.

June 17, 1978

Neal accused me of being a bad mother today. Carmella was weeping in her crib as Elsa had a temper tantrum in the kitchen, and I just couldn't keep up with both of them at once. He came home in the midst of all of that, and I swear, at that moment, I almost told him what I was up to, that I was in love with someone else. I tried to imagine what his eyes would do when he found out. Would he feel ashamed? Would he hate me?

Before I could decide what to say to him, he stormed up to his room and turned on the television. I wanted to laugh myself silly. Why did I marry a man who looks at me like I'm his slave? Who impregnated me and then left me in his house to rot?

Feeling abused and neglected, I finally put Carmella down and got Elsa to sleep. And then, enraged, I called Oliver and asked if he wanted to meet. Oliver was frightened at first, but then, he was game. The babysitter came over immediately, and I was out the door, flying off to see Oliver—this time at his apartment rather than the hotel. I no longer cared who knew.

On the back porch of the house that Carmella shared with Cody, she sighed as she closed her mother's journal and pressed it against her heart. Never had she imagined such angst in her mother's life. Never had she imagined such sorrow. Back in the house, Cody entered the front door and called her name, and Carmella said, "I'm back here!" Cody appeared on the porch a moment later, his smile the most nourishing thing she knew.

"What are you doing back here?" Cody asked, eyeing Georgia's bassinet in the shadows of the porch where she slept.

"We're enjoying the beautiful weather," Carmella said, blinking back tears.

Cody kissed Carmella on the cheek and then walked over to his baby, gazing down at her with love in his eyes. Carmella thought about the stark comparison between Cody and Neal, two fathers who operated the mechanics of fatherhood very differently. Her heart lifted.

"Cody?"

"Yeah?" He turned to smile at her.

"I know we just had Georgia," she began, "so don't worry if it's a no. But I was wondering if you'd consider having another baby. I wouldn't mind trying for a boy."

Cody's smile widened with surprise. "A boy."

Carmella stood and walked toward him, her arms wrapping around his torso. How could she tell him that ever since they'd lost Colton, she'd dreamed of having a little boy as a baby, one she could raise and protect the way she hadn't been able to protect Colton?

"I'm forty-five," Carmella breathed, "and I'm not getting any younger. But the doctor said I still have a few good years. And I'd like to use them if you're okay with that."

Cody pressed his nose against hers. "I think we'd better get started."

Carmella laughed and kissed him, trying to drown out her mother's long-ago sorrow with her own happiness. Although she was curious about her mother's affair and how it had ended, she couldn't help but fear that her mother's sorrow was infecting her current life here. And she didn't want any of it.

Chapter Nine

After that night at the bar, when Cole had laughed himself silly with the young woman in the miniskirt, Aria didn't see Cole for a little while. He didn't stop by the bar and only texted her occasionally with a funny video or song he thought she might like. There was no sense that he wanted to know how she was or to see her. And through each and every aching day alone, Aria felt abandoned.

It didn't help that that week was meant to be Aria's graduation from Savannah College of Art and Design. On various social media channels, she watched the students who'd ridiculed her work, called it bad and derivative, pose with diplomas and family members, smiling happily as they committed themselves to the next era of their architecture lives. In a few photographs, Professor Judah Heskew posed as well, smiling in a way that made Aria feel betrayed. She hadn't written him back once since she'd left spontaneously last semester, but that didn't mean she didn't think about him, about architecture, and about her future. She was at a standstill.

Wednesday afternoon, Aria said goodbye to Carmella after a few hours of babysitting and drove to the bar with the windows down and the radio turned up. As she drove, she sang along, making up lyrics as she went as the breeze off the Nantucket Sound blew through her blonde hair.

To her surprise, Cole sat outside the bar, his face lifted to take in the sun. Aria studied him as she walked toward the door to unlock it, stirring with fear. Maybe Cole had come to the bar to tell her that he'd gotten involved with that woman from the other night. Maybe he finally wanted to confess that he was tired of their weird game of cat and mouse and that he was ready to settle down with someone who made more sense to him.

"Hi!" Cole's eyes opened with surprise when he heard her approach.

Against her better judgment, Aria felt herself smile. "Hi, stranger."

Cole popped up and followed her into the shadowed bar, where she placed her things on the counter and began to take chairs off the tables. Cole followed her lead, just as he had many times before, helping her between his shifts out at sea.

"I haven't heard from you," Cole said, his tone difficult to read.

Aria raised her eyebrows. "I've been busy."

Cole nodded, his hands wrapped around two legs of a chair. "You work too much."

"I'm not sure about that." Aria shot him a look.

Cole was quiet for a moment. "Did you like that song I sent you the other day?"

"Which one?"

"The one by the band Television."

Aria pretended to think for a moment, when in reality, she'd listened to the song ten times and cried herself to sleep to it. "Maybe. I think I liked it."

Cole smiled slightly, then positioned the final stool along the bar. Aria couldn't understand why he looked at her like that, as though he was a puppy dog. She walked around the bar and glared at him, wanting to demand what was going on. Maybe the girl in the miniskirt had abandoned him.

"Do you want to get pizza later?" Cole asked, palming the back of his neck.

Aria shrugged. "Do you?"

Cole dropped his gaze, clearly disappointed. Aria wavered between wanting to show how hurt she'd been and wanting to throw herself over the bar and hug him.

But before she could do either of those things, Aria found herself tugging the mysterious envelope from her back pocket and placing it on the counter between them. "I got this in the mail. No return address. It's really weird."

Cole frowned and removed the newspaper clipping from within.

"It's my mom," Aria explained, pointing to the young woman in the photograph. "But she never told me she went to my university nor that she was an architect. I've never even heard her mention she liked the look of a building!"

Cole furrowed his brow, curious. "Did you call and ask her about it?"

Aria blushed. "We're not really talking." The truth was that Aria just wasn't up to talking to her mother, not after everything that had happened. "I researched online, but there's nothing."

"I bet they have records at the university," Cole said simply.

"Yeah. But what would I get out of seeing them? Just more proof that my mother was withholding information from me all these years?"

"I don't know," Cole said. "Don't you want to see what your mom used to work on? Who she used to be before she became a mother?"

Aria softened at the sentiment. In truth, she'd never really gotten to know who her mother was behind the dark shadow of her father, who ruled everything.

"I haven't been back to campus since before the sailing trip," Aria said.

"Weren't you supposed to..." Cole trailed off, not sure if he should finish.

"Yeah. I was supposed to graduate last weekend," Aria muttered. "I feel conflicted about the whole thing, to tell you the truth."

Aria's heart swelled at the admittance. It was a rare thing for her to tell anyone the truth.

Cole's face broke open with his smile. "I'm up for an adventure if you are."

"What do you mean?" Aria gaped at him.

"Savannah is just down the coast."

"It's not just down the coast. It's way down there," Aria said. "And I haven't been back on a boat since everything that happened."

Cole waved his hand. "I promise that what happened in the Caribbean won't happen again. The circumstances are different now. And it'll just be the two of us. We can stop when we're tired and sleep in whatever harbor we please."

What Cole described was perhaps the most romantic

expedition Aria had ever heard of. She peered into his eyes, trying to find something in there— something that proved he loved her. But after seven months of seeing one another nearly every day, she felt even further from being able to read him than ever before.

"I have to work," Aria heard herself protest.

"Ask for it off," Cole insisted, then lowered his voice, glancing around. "And, Aria. It's not like your future is in this bar, anyway. Don't cling to it."

Aria knew he was right.

That evening, she requested a week off of work and called Carmella to ensure she had a babysitter to cover her shifts. When Carmella asked Aria where she was headed, Aria explained, "Cole and I are going on a sailing trip," and Carmella shrieked with excitement.

"I'm sorry," Carmella said. "It just sounds so romantic."

"We're just friends," Aria corrected, her cheeks burning.

"Right. I know that. But being out in the wind and the sun, surrounded by all that ocean, sounds romantic. That's all I mean," Carmella said hurriedly.

To pack for their trip, Cole and Alyssa set aside an afternoon to shop for groceries and tend to Cole's sailboat, which needed to be cleaned for such a big journey. Throughout that day, as the sun beat down upon them and Cole's radio played the top hits of another decade, Aria and Cole swept, scrubbed, and assembled the sleeping area, where they would sleep after they docked in various harbors as they journeyed south. At one point, when the heat lifted into the low eighties, Cole removed his shirt and wrapped a handkerchief around his head, and Aria thought she might swoon off the boat.

Aria was sure she'd never been in love with someone the way she was now in love with Cole. Because she was a Baldwin, she'd gone to all of the most prestigious boarding schools growing up, which had allowed her father to brag about his prestige through his children's status and education. Aria had detested almost everyone at every boarding school to the point that she'd been crippled with loneliness and often acted out. Still, she'd kept her grades up and graduated in the top ten of her class, which hadn't mattered to her father. He'd only cared about the name of the boarding school.

Aria was now twenty-four years old, nearly twenty-five, and falling in love like this felt strange. It felt calm, peaceful, and wonderful, like a tide slowly coming over her. Previous "crushes" had been very different, like lightning bolts that had struck her, dropping her to the pavement.

Aria slept over at Cole's place on the night before they left. They ate pizza and watched bad television, making fun of the characters as they made silly decisions. Aria donned one of Cole's t-shirts and slept on the couch, her heart bubbling with expectation. And when she awoke and made coffee, they sat together in a sunbeam and chatted about their next days together.

Aria was slightly apprehensive about the boat ride. It was true that the night back in October in the Caribbean had been a nightmare for her, something that had rocked her psyche. But as Cole expertly glided the sailboat away from the coast, Aria lifted her eyes to the horizon and felt the Atlantic winds across her face, and she dreamed about a version of herself that was brave enough to live beyond her fears.

That first night, they latched their boat to a very slow

and empty harbor, a six-hour sail away from Martha's Vineyard. There, they got out and stretched their legs, wandering through a cute little town and grabbing some Italian food. Cole ordered spaghetti, and Aria ordered lasagna, which was mercifully quite cheap given the non-touristy nature of the town. They also ordered a bottle of wine. Aria couldn't help but think that nearly everyone else at the restaurant, all of whom were locals, probably assumed they were a couple. *Didn't they look like it?*

As Cole raised a forkful of spaghetti to his lips, he locked eyes with her and asked, "Why do you think your mom never told you that she went to Savannah College?"

Aria sighed and set down her fork. "My mother and I have never told each other anything."

"Why do you think that is?"

Aria raised her eyebrows. "I think she's afraid of what she'll say when she tries to tell the truth."

"I feel like you're a pretty honest person," Cole said. "It's strange that you're so different than your mother."

Aria felt this was terribly ironic, given the fact that she could never tell Cole what was on her mind.

"I don't know if I'm that honest," Aria said simply.

"Have you ever lied to me?" Cole asked, his eyes glinting.

Aria stuck her tongue into the inside of her cheek. "What a question," she teased after a moment. *Was he flirting with her?*

"I mean," Cole began, leaning slightly over the table, "you are a woman of mystery."

Aria laughed and sipped her wine, overwhelmed by his attention. "I don't know about that."

"Come on, Aria. You appeared out of nowhere on the island in the middle of a dark and stormy night," Cole said. "And now, you've been part of Martha's Vineyard life for six months?"

"Seven."

"And I still have no idea what you think of it. Of your life there. Or why you left your life in Savannah behind," Cole finished.

Aria took another drink of wine, thinking she could have probably drunk the entire bottle just to get out of this conversation. After a small pause, Aria managed to say, "You met my family. We're a confusing bunch. I never really felt like I belonged to them. Actually, I never felt like I belonged anywhere."

Cole nodded as though he understood, but how could he? His parents had always loved him. He'd always been accepted.

"Any idea who could have sent you this newspaper clip?" Cole asked.

Aria shook her head.

"Could it be your mother? Trying to send you a message?"

"It wasn't her handwriting," Aria insisted. "And my mother is way too secretive for something like this. I don't know! I honestly don't."

Cole smiled. "Then it's a good thing we're getting to the bottom of it together. I feel like we're spies or something."

Aria blushed and stared down at her lasagna, hardly capable of believing any of this was real. "I'm nervous about being back in Savannah."

Cole tilted his head. "Why?"

"Nobody liked me there. I felt so strange."

Cole placed his hand over Aria's on the table, and

Aria's skin beneath his hand felt like fire. "I'll be there with you the entire time. You don't have to worry."

Aria raised her eyes to his, overwhelmed by the power of his friendship. "That means a lot to me, Cole. Really."

Cole removed his hand, and Aria wanted to scream at him to put it back. "It's my pleasure. And isn't this Italian place great? It's a little hole in the wall that my dad always took me to when we went on longer sailing trips together. He always swore it was the best of the best on the east coast, and I have to say I agree with him."

Aria's heart swelled at the image of Cole with his father, perhaps even at this very table— Cole youthful and bright-eyed as his father recalled beautiful sailing stories, walking Cole through the adventures of his life. Aria had a sense that Cole would have similar stories. Maybe he would one day sit with someone and tell the story of when he brought a very silly, lost young woman back to Savannah to learn the hidden secrets of her mother's past. Maybe he would tell them, "She was such a mysterious woman. I never understood her at all."

Chapter Ten

Carmella returned to her mother's diary late that night after feeding Georgia. The moon illuminated one end of the couch, and she wiggled her toes in it, thinking about Tina Remington so many years ago, destroying her marriage with every decision, with reckless and romantic abandon. What would Carmella have thought of that woman? Would she have appreciated how much she listened to her heart? Would she have loved her joie de vivre?

August 5, 1978

Oliver asked me to meet him at a mysterious address. After the babysitter arrived, I drove out to an area of the island I didn't know well and peered through the trees to find his car tucked in beside a little stone cottage by the ocean. I couldn't make sense of it. I drove up beside his car and then found him on the cottage's back porch, gazing out across the ocean as though he was a very old man and not thirty-five years old. I laughed at him and kissed him, so grateful to be back in his arms. Sometimes, I tell myself that we can't choose when we meet the right people. They come when we least expect them.

"Oliver. What is this place?" I asked him, flabbergasted.

And he brought forward two keys, both glinting in the summer light, and told me he'd just purchased this place "for us." I could hardly believe it. I took the key and then kissed him, hardly able to understand what he's done for us — that he'd taken this first step toward building a world for us.

It goes without saying what we did after that, in every room of the house. I told him I loved him in every room, and he blushed the way he does, as though he can't handle the intensity of my emotions. He's not my therapist anymore, after all. He's tied up in the mess of me.

It was getting late. Oliver cooked us a pasta dinner, which we ate outside, watching the water roll across the sands. For the first time, Oliver asked me what I thought about leaving Neal. "People get divorced all the time, Tina." I don't know why, but this made me cry.

August 7, 1978

I'm writing this entry on the back porch of the stone cottage Oliver bought to house our secret affair. Oliver is in the kitchen, putting together a salad, and it's struck me, as I sit here, listening to the waves, that Oliver is the only man who'd ever cooked for me. Why is it such a rare thing to feel cared for, especially if you're a woman? I don't think any of my friends' husbands do anything regarding meals. I don't think they even pick up apples at the store or grab a six-pack of beer.

Oliver hasn't asked me again about Neal or whether I would consider leaving him, but I can see the question lurking behind his eyes. I suppose by now, so many months after we began the affair, we must ask ourselves these questions. Why would Oliver stay with me if I'm unwilling to make an enormous sacrifice? Why would he always want to remain a secret?

I've considered what my peers of Martha's Vineyard will say if Oliver and I go through with it. What will they call me? Neal Remington is so beloved, and the Vineyard looks to the Katama Lodge and Wellness Spa with endless pride. Will my affair with Oliver belittle Neal's reputation? Then again, there's a chance it could bolster it, with so many feeling "so sorry for poor Neal." And I imagine it wouldn't take Neal long to find a second wife.

It's also true that Neal wasn't always this way toward me. Initially, he was sweet, talking endlessly about starting his Lodge and building a family with me. I got all wrapped up in that love almost too tightly, which is why I feel mystified now that I've gone years without feeling any love from Neal. Where did that love go?

August 10, 1978

Today, out of the blue, the babysitter called to say she couldn't watch Carmella and Elsa. You would have thought she'd called to say the world was ending— that was how devastating it was. I cried about being unable to come over to the little cottage by the sea.

But then, Oliver called me and said, "Why don't you just bring them with you?"

At first, I said this wasn't possible, as though the watchful eyes of my children would immediately clue Neal into what I'm doing. But then I thought— why the heck not? I'm on the verge of asking for a divorce anyway, and my children are still very young. Carmella can't speak, and Neal isn't around Elsa enough to catch wind of any "new friends" she might have.

So, here I am on the back porch of the seaside cottage with both of my daughters. Carmella is fast asleep in her carrier, and Elsa is at the porch table with Oliver, drawing pictures. I realize I've never seen Oliver with a child before, and the image makes my heart shatter with longing. I want that man's child. I want to go the distance with him.

Before I return to the Remington House tonight, I'll tell Oliver it's time. It's time that I tell Neal the truth and devise a plan to get out of that marriage. Neal probably won't want to care for the children even half of the time, which means that Carmella, Elsa, and I will move here with Oliver, and Oliver will have to play the role of a step-father. I know it will be a wonderful fit.

August 13, 1978

I know it's reckless, but I've just called Neal at the Lodge to tell him I won't be coming home tonight. A lie came out of me before I could stop it— that I'm staying at a friend's place with both girls. At first, he was mystified, as I've never done anything like that before. His voice became very meek, and he asked, "Have I done something wrong? Are you leaving me?" And I couldn't bring myself to tell him, not then. I was petrified. So, I told him that it had gotten late here, that both Elsa and Carmella were asleep, and that I didn't want to wake them up to move them. He understood, then he even got a bit excited. He loves having nights to himself. I wonder what he does with his time.

But now, Elsa and Carmella are asleep in the guest room (what I've secretly begun to refer to as their room), and I'm in bed, listening to the stream of water as Oliver showers. A warmth of happiness is flooding through me, and I know it's too late to stop it.

I suppose if I never saw Neal again, I would be fine with that.

* * *

Carmella woke early the next morning to a kiss on her forehead. Her eyes fluttered open to find Cody above her, smiling gently.

"You never came back to bed," he whispered.

Carmella stretched her arms over her head, hovering between dreamland and waking life, and said, "I was reading. I must have fallen asleep."

Cody went into the kitchen to make a pot of coffee, and Carmella walked back into their bedroom to try to sleep as much as possible. It was a little past nine when she woke, and Georgia needed to be changed and fed. As Carmella performed the tasks easily and happily, she thought of her mother and Oliver in that sea cottage, pretending to be the couple raising little Elsa and Carmella. It was wild to Carmella that wherever this cottage was, she and Elsa had been to it, had sat out on the back porch and felt the breeze through their hair.

Elsa texted a little before noon to see if Carmella had lunch plans. They agreed to meet at a place with to-die-for fish of the day and gorgeous salads on a street lined with historic Victorian homes in Edgartown. Carmella showered and did her makeup for the first time in a few days, then set Georgia up in her carrier and got out the door. At the restaurant, she was a little bit early and sat in the fresh light of the deck with Georgia beside her, protected beneath the umbrella.

"There they are! My favorite girls." Elsa strode across the deck in a linen jumpsuit, smiling.

Carmella jumped up to hug her sister, complimenting her new perfume as she sat back down.

"You look wonderful. Well-rested, even," Elsa said.

"Georgia and I have found a pretty good rhythm," Carmella confessed. "But I know that rhythm can change at any time."

Carmella and Elsa ordered fish, salads, and lemonade, then caught one another up on the basics of their lives. Apparently, Maggie and Alyssa were still living at the Remington House and were both still pregnant. "Maggie is constantly stress-baking and bringing the baked goods to The Dog-Eared Corner, and Alyssa is constantly eating as many of the baked goods as she can get her hands on."

"Is Alyssa showing?"

"Not quite," Elsa said. "I imagine it'll happen some-time this summer."

Carmella sipped her lemonade, remembering the real gossip of the week. "We haven't even talked about Cole and Aria's big adventure!"

"I know." Elsa dropped her voice to a whisper. "When he told me that he and Aria were going to sail to Savannah, I nearly dropped the phone."

"What do you think it means? Do you think they're together?"

Elsa shrugged. "What do I know? But it's a long time to be on such a tiny boat with another person. I bet if you and Cody had been on an adventure like that at their age, you would have admitted your true feelings a lot earlier."

Carmella laughed. "Have you heard from him since they left?"

"He texted that they finally arrived in Savannah," Elsa explained. "He sent a photograph, too. It looks beau-tiful down there."

Carmella took Elsa's phone and gazed at the photograph of the beautiful and very old city, a place she'd never been, its streets lined with moss-filled trees.

And then, as Carmella passed the phone across the table, she heard herself ask something she thought she never would.

"Do you remember Mom ever talking about someone named Oliver?"

Elsa took her phone and pocketed it, her eyebrows dropping. "Oliver? Oliver, who?"

"Oliver Matthews," Carmella explained, losing confidence. "He was a therapist here on the island back in the late seventies, I guess. And maybe even later."

Elsa shook her head.

"What about Dad? He never mentioned anyone by that name?" Carmella pushed it.

"Not that I remember. Why? Where did you hear that name?"

Carmella's cheeks burned with fear. A very small yet loud part of her yearned to tell Elsa what she'd learned in the diary about this man who'd set their mother's heart on fire. Yet the rest of her knew how much this news would destroy Elsa's perfect vision of their parents' love.

"I could look him up online?" Elsa raised her phone and waved it.

"No. Don't bother." Carmella took a fish bite, smiling as though the Oliver Matthews question had been a blip. Then, she asked, "So, what do you think Aria and Cole's babies are going to look like?" Elsa threw her head back, howling.

They were back on track.

Chapter Eleven

The Historic Thomas House was located just three blocks from the Savannah College of Art and Design architecture building, a three-story home that was rumored to be haunted. For years, Aria had walked past with her backpack, engaging with the beauty of the pillars, the big windows, and the burnt-orange bricks, which made the place look like it was out of a fairy tale. When Cole had asked where Aria wanted to stay during their stint in Savannah, she'd said the house's name almost without thought.

And now, she and Cole stood in front of it, their chins lifted to take it in. They'd been sailing three days in total, stopping in little ports and harbors to rest, drink wine, and talk the nights away, both swimming in one another's eyes as the moonlight hung over whichever bay they'd stopped in for the night.

At the front desk of the bed and breakfast, a woman named Rhonda told them they were in luck. Due to most of the students leaving for the summer semester and their families not visiting, they still had a room available in the bed and breakfast.

"It's a queen-sized bed," Rhonda explained as she checked her computer. "How does that sound?"

Aria's throat tightened as she glanced at Cole. Cole did not look at her. Throughout their journey and even their friendship, they hadn't slept in the same bed even once.

"That should be fine," Cole finally said, still not looking at Aria.

A wave of fear and excitement fell over Aria. They told Rhonda they wanted to stay for at least two days, maybe three, and Rhonda took their information down with a ballpoint pen and then gave them a pamphlet informing them about Savannah— where to eat and where to explore.

The room itself was ornate, with enormous windows and floral wallpaper. The queen-sized bed was a four-poster, and Cole jumped up on it, crossed his ankles, and leaned against the luxurious pillows.

"After sleeping in the boat for a few days, a real bed always feels so dang good," he said, his eyes wistful.

Aria had to stop herself from jumping onto the bed with him and wrapping her arms around him.

They decided to shower, change, and then head to the architecture offices before they closed at five that afternoon. Aria paid extra attention to her makeup and hair, beautifying herself in a way she hadn't since before she'd left Savannah last September. At the time, she'd been exhausted, at the edge of her creative spirit and unsure if she could draw anything worthy of the university. Around her, the other students had seemed so sure of themselves, opening themselves up to their creativity with a courage Aria couldn't comprehend.

When Aria had told one of the students that she planned to go on a vacation with her family but work from the sailboat, he had scoffed and said, "You're not coming back. I can see it in your eyes." Aria had often wondered how he'd known.

Aria and Cole waved goodbye to Rhonda and stepped out onto the front porch of the historic bed and breakfast, ready to face the world. As they walked along the tree-lined boulevards, moss shifted dreamily in the soft breeze, and Aria's fingers briefly swept across Cole's.

"This place is magical," Cole said. "It must have inspired you to make beautiful architecture."

Aria crossed her arms over her chest. "It did, at first. I thought I was going to become someone special in the world of architecture." She paused at a stop sign to watch several cars burst past, then added, "I was really naive."

Cole arched his eyebrow. "It's not naive to think you can make something special. Something that could change the world in a small yet significant way."

Aria met Cole's gaze and shivered once more at the energy behind his eyes. *What on earth was he thinking about? Why could she never guess it?*

Outside the architecture building, Aria took a deep breath, stepped through the massive, heavy wooden door, and led Cole to the front office. The woman behind the front desk blinked at Aria and smiled without recognition. Aria had probably spoken to the woman upward of ten times, and the lack of friendliness felt like a smack in the face. But then again, Aria hadn't been back on campus since September of last year.

"Good afternoon! Can I help you with something?"

Aria placed her hands on the smooth wood of the front desk. "I was curious if you have any records regarding the graduating classes of 1994, 1995, and 1996."

The woman raised her eyebrows curiously. "We have graduating records, yes. We also have graduation projects from all classes dating back to the seventies."

The woman led Aria to a back room, wherein they stored files upon files from architecture students from previous years. She pointed out the drawers that included information from the mid-nineties, then said, "We close up at five, and we don't allow any files to be taken from the premises. You can always come back tomorrow if you don't find what you need."

With a shivering hand, Aria selected one of the folders from 1994 and began to parse through the pages. Cole stood directly behind her, watching her flip. Names and dates whizzed past, none of them familiar.

"What's your mother's name again?" Cole opened a drawer filled with documents from 1995 and rifled through.

"Her maiden name was Quinn. Bethany Quinn," Aria explained as she slid 1994 back into its slot.

Cole flipped open the new folder, his eyes widening. "I think this is it."

Aria hurried over to see a list of the graduates from 1995, which included Bethany Quinn. Her heart dropped into her stomach as she flipped through the pages to find photographs of architecture functions and even graded assignments. Apparently, her mother had written an essay about Prague's architecture, which required her to study abroad for three months during the autumn of 1994. A photograph of Bethany Quinn as a young woman in Prague was included in the file, her arms slung over the shoulders of other architecture students. Her smile was open, genuine, and far happier than Aria had ever seen.

The essay was included. Aria skimmed the first few lines, engaging with her mother's words. Cole watched her as she read and finally commented, "It must be something special."

"It is," Aria affirmed as she wiped a tear from her cheek. "I can't remember ever reading anything my mother ever wrote. It makes me feel so strange. Why didn't she ever tell me she came here? Why was her big architecture past a secret?"

Cole shrugged. "Did something happen here? Something that hurt her?"

Aria continued to scan the artifacts within the folder, unsure how to answer Cole's question. In her mind, Bethany Baldwin had always wanted to live within the shadow of Kenny Baldwin. She'd wanted children, a big house in Texas, and enough money to brag to their friends about. When had Bethany Quinn transitioned to Bethany Baldwin? When had she given up on herself? And had giving up on herself like that been worth it?

Toward the very back of the folder were more photographs taken from this iconic trip to Prague. Her mother was featured in many of them, her hand around a big beer and her eyes dancing. In one of them, a darker one at a Prague dive bar, Aria first recognized the man directly beside Bethany in the photograph.

"Oh my gosh." Aria's mouth fell open.

"What?" Cole hurried around her to look at the photograph, then shook his head. "What do you see?"

At the old wooden table in a long-forgotten bar sat

Bethany Quinn, beautiful, blond, terribly bright, and happy, alongside a man with a scraggly beard, thick-rimmed glasses, and a wool sweater. In the photograph, he gazed at Bethany adoringly as though she had all the secrets of the world.

"I know that man."

"Who is he? He looks like he's crazy in love with your mom."

Aria's throat tightened. *It couldn't be, could it?*

"He's a professor here at Savannah College of Art and Design," Aria continued. "Professor Judah Heskew."

"Was he a professor back when your mom was going here?" Cole asked.

Aria checked the list of graduating seniors again to find that Judah Heskew had graduated alongside her mother in 1995. Aria remembered that Judah had said he'd been a student here, that it had been his pleasure to return to his alma mater as a professor. But she never could have imagined that he'd known her mother.

And then, the realization hit her like a bag of bricks.

Professor Judah Heskew had always known Aria was Bethany Quinn's daughter.

But why hadn't he said he'd known Aria's mother back in the day? Why had he kept it a secret?

Aria sat on a dusty stool, her head swimming with intrigue.

Suddenly, the woman from the front desk popped her head in to say it was now five o'clock, and they needed to exit the premises. Aria gaped at her, genuinely shocked that so much time had passed. Quickly, she took photographs of her mother and Professor Heskew and the list of graduating seniors from 1995. Then, she and Cole burst from the records office and into the exhilarating light of another late afternoon in Savannah.

For a long time, Aria remained wordless, her thoughts humming. Almost without thought, she led Cole to a bar she'd once frequented, sat at the bar counter, and ordered herself a pint. Her mind was heavy with the image of her own mother with a beer in Prague, her eyes dancing at something Professor Heskew had said. Cole ordered himself a beer, as well, and remained quiet, scanning the decorations around the bar. Unlike other bars in the area, this one had no televisions and upheld the old city's history. Newspapers were hung in frames, protected by glass, and long candles were lit, melting into mountains of wax.

Suddenly, Cole placed his hand on Aria's shoulder. The touch was so powerful that Aria nearly leaped from her skin.

"Aria? Are you all right?" Cole's voice was very quiet and sincere.

Aria sipped her beer. "I just can't figure any of it out." She realized, as she said it, that she meant two things at once: her mother's secrecy and her relationship with Cole. *What did any of it mean?*

"You know that professor well?"

Aria nodded. "He took me under his wing when I first got here. I was a bit older than the other students, and I never really felt like I fit in, you know? I found myself chatting with him at an architecture function. I liked his jokes, and he liked mine. Around that time, I showed him my initial sketches, and he went crazy for them. He told me I had some kind of 'singular vision' or whatever." Aria bit her lip. "Now, I'm wondering if that was all a ruse just to get to my mom. I mean, all the other students thought I was a hack, anyway."

"There's no way you got into this school as a hack," Cole pointed out.

Aria shrugged. "My self-esteem around architecture is already pretty low. But I never imagined this. Professor Heskew even wrote me a few times over the past few months, asking if I'd consider returning to school."

"There's no way he would do that just for a woman he maybe had a crush on back in 1995," Cole insisted. "He genuinely believes in you."

But Aria wasn't so sure. Wordless, she sipped the rest of her beer, then paid for both of their drinks and hurried into the evening air. Cole kept up with her, following her into the next bar down the road, one that was a bit rowdier than the candlelit one.

"Aria, we should really eat something," Cole said, his eyes shimmering with worry. "I don't mind having a few drinks, but there's no reason we should go crazy."

Aria refused to look him in the eye. She ordered herself a beer and sat at the counter, surveying the other bar revelers, some of whom she half-recognized from her years at the university.

And then, out of nowhere, Julia walked through the front door. She was one of the students Aria had heard talking badly about her architecture work last August before she'd officially dropped out.

"Aria Baldwin? Is that really you?" Her smile was enormous, almost genuine. She hurried over and hugged Aria, who remained stiff and unyielding. "We thought you dropped off the face of the earth!"

Aria sipped her beer, unsure what to do with this information. "I guess I didn't."

Julia laughed and ordered a beer. "Are you going back next semester? I'll be around, getting my master's."

"That's nice."

Julia gazed at Cole, a look of confusion marring her face. "My name is Julia. I was in Aria's class in architecture school before she dropped out." Julia feigned concern, adding, "We really were so sad you didn't return from your little sailing adventure. You're a Baldwin, so we know it isn't necessary that you get a job in anything. But you are so talented, Aria."

Aria wanted to remind Julia that she'd spoken at length about Aria's lack of talent just last year, but she decided it wasn't worth it.

"You were missed at graduation," Julia continued, as though she just couldn't stop. "We had a big party and everything. Professor Judah gave a speech that made me cry."

When Aria didn't answer back, Julia returned her attention to Cole. Her eyes glinted flirtatiously. "Are you also a college dropout?"

"I never made it to college," Cole answered.

"Oh? And what have you been doing with yourself if you're not on a quest for knowledge?" Julia asked.

"I'm a sailor," Cole explained.

Julia's smile widened, and she slid onto the stool beside Cole. Aria recognized her eyes— they looked just like the eyes of the young woman in the miniskirt back in Martha's Vineyard, the one who'd been so obvious about wanting Cole.

"Tell me. Where do you sail?" Julia asked.

Cole answered easily, as though he didn't notice how interested in him Julia already was. "I mostly sail around

Martha's Vineyard. Last summer, I was working in the Caribbean, which is how I met Aria."

"Oh! Is that why our Aria never came back?" Julia asked.

Cole glanced at Aria. "Aria has plenty of reasons that have nothing to do with sailing."

Julia laughed, as though she hadn't heard what Cole said. "Did you sail to Savannah?"

"Yeah," Cole said. "It was nice to do a longer journey again."

"I would love to be out there," Julia said. "On the open water! Wow. It must feel exhilarating."

Aria's stomach twisted itself into knots. As Cole and Aria chatted, she ordered herself another beer, considering what to do with herself now that Cole was clearly flirting with one of her nemeses.

A few minutes later, Julia went to the bathroom, turned, and asked, "Save my seat, Cole?" Afterward, Cole turned back to find Aria deep in her next beer, her eyes glazed.

"Hey! You want to go?" Cole asked.

Aria shrugged flippantly. She wanted to scream.

"Are you having a bad time?"

"No, Cole. I'm having a fantastic time," Aria shot back flatly. "It's so nice to reconnect with old classmates."

"Julia says you're really talented. I knew it."

Aria turned to glare at Cole, genuinely at a loss. "I'm not."

"I'm sure you are," Cole insisted.

Suddenly, Julia returned to the bar, all smiley, as though she'd been formed from glitter. Aria placed a ten-dollar bill on the counter and told the bartender she was out as Cole's smile fell off his face.

"Where are you going?"

"I'll meet you back in the room," Aria said. "Stay out. You're having fun."

Before Cole could answer, Aria stormed out of the bar as tears slid down her cheeks. She felt foolish and youthful. When she reached the bed and breakfast, she stomped upstairs, donned a big t-shirt, and curled into a ball beneath the sheets. For a long time, she remained like that, quivering with sorrow.

Chapter Twelve

Georgia fell asleep soundly that night and left Carmella in the silence of herself, her head stirring with questions about her mother's past. In the next room, Cody read quietly, sipping tea and eating a cookie as a soft rain flattened across the window-panes. Both petrified and eager to learn more, Carmella grabbed her mother's diary and flipped to the next page, prepared to read.

August 20, 1978

I tried to tell Neal today. We sat together peacefully on the back porch, watching the sun drop into the western horizon. Carmella was sound asleep in her crib, and Elsa was asleep in her bedroom. For a moment, as Neal looked at me across the table, I remembered how we'd once been with one another: genuinely happy and excited to build a future together. At this moment, I thought, "I need to be honest with him." But the moment passed very quickly. Neal jumped up to grab himself a beer, and then he began to talk about the Lodge again (there's always something to say about the Lodge). I spent the next two hours nodding along, my head swimming with thoughts of Oliver.

August 21, 1978

Oliver is beginning to lose patience. I can feel it when he holds me, as though he's at the edge of his rope and is preparing to leave me if I can't find it within myself to leave my husband. I feel too weak for him. A part of me wants to ask him why he doesn't leave the island and go off and find someone else— someone who isn't married with two little children. But then, when we make love, I know in my heart that he's the only one for me. He's the man I want to change my life for.

This afternoon, we're at our house by the sea. Oliver is making pasta while I write this, and he's whistling to himself as, on the radio, someone is talking about the weather. Miraculously, I don't have Elsa or Carmella today, and there's such freedom in being alone with Oliver without any sense of obligation.

Cody appeared in the doorway between the kitchen and the living room, smiling sweetly. "Do you want some popcorn?"

Carmella closed her mother's diary and followed Cody into the kitchen, her head humming with thoughts of her mother, who seemed on the brink of telling Carmella's father she was going to leave. It hadn't worked out. What then had transpired?

As Carmella watched Cody prepare the popcorn and melt butter on the stovetop, she allowed herself a moment to consider what it would feel like to learn that Cody had had an affair. *Would she find a way to forgive him? Or would she tell him to leave her and their baby forever?* The thought felt alien to her, especially given how in love they were, but she wasn't naive. People cheated on people all the time. People fell out of love.

"Have you ever had a friend who cheated on their partner?" Carmella asked.

Cody gave her a look. "Should I be worried?"

Carmella laughed and waved her hand. "Not in the slightest. I'm just thinking."

Cody shook the popcorn kernels on the stovetop as the first few burst at the bottom. "A guy at work cheated on his wife with another woman at work. It was a terrible scandal. The new relationship didn't work out, and their marriages broke up."

Carmella frowned. "Did they seem happy during the affair?"

"Everyone knew about it," Cody answered. "Some women at the office considered telling the wronged partners about the affair. I think they saw their lack of honesty as a direct attack against their relationships."

"That's a bit selfish, isn't it? I mean, not everyone else's decision is about you," Carmella said.

"I thought the same," Cody affirmed. "I don't condone cheating. But I never thought for a second that because Billy at work was cheating on his wife, that had anything to do with me, you, or anything in my life."

Carmella nodded, her head stirring with questions.

"What's on your mind?" Cody asked, frowning.

Carmella gestured vaguely toward the living room. After a dramatic pause, she said, "My mother was cheating on my father."

Cody's eyes widened. "Really? You read that in the diary?"

"The entire diary is basically a record of how much my

mother loved her therapist," Carmella continued. "She used to take Elsa and I to a seaside cottage to see him. It's hard to wrap my mind around it, especially because I know the affair doesn't work out. I just don't know how it falls apart yet."

"It's a ticking time bomb," Cody agreed. "Does it hurt to read these stories?"

"No," Carmella answered honestly. "It seems like my father was not the easiest man to live with, and Oliver offered my mother a great deal of kindness and love. It seems natural that she would open her heart to that."

"I imagine Elsa doesn't feel the same."

Carmella grimaced. "I haven't told her."

"Are you going to?"

"I have no idea." Carmella sighed, watching as the popcorn kernels burst and bounced against the glass lid of the pot. "She loved Dad so much, and I know that memories of him help her through her grief. The truth could be a detriment to that."

Carmella returned to the couch with a bowl of popcorn, eager to keep reading. But the next entry in the diary came a week after the previous, a gap that wasn't normal for Tina Remington at the height of her affair.

August 31, 1978

I hardly know how to write this down.

But I suppose it must be recorded, just as I've recorded everything else.

I had plans to meet Oliver at the seaside cottage last week. I had the girls with me. Carmella was asleep, and Elsa and I played little games on the porch, waiting. Oliver was late, which was strange. I decided to wait for him for a half-hour before I called his office. His secretary said he was off today.

After two hours of waiting, I had to get the girls back

home. I was outraged, but more than that, I was frightened. I began to think that Oliver was about to leave me. That he'd met someone else or that he was too tired of waiting around for me.

I returned home to make dinner for Neal. I was in a terrible mood, making a lot of noise in the kitchen. As the beans boiled in the pot, a neighbor down the road called, and I answered it angrily.

"Have you heard the news?" our neighbor, Mrs. Talmon, asked me.

"What news?" I practically bit her head off.

"That therapist of yours," Mrs. Talmon went on. "He was in a boating accident last night."

I nearly toppled to the floor after that. I hardly remember what she told me and had to piece it together later when more people called me to gossip about it. The gist is that Oliver went on a sailing trip last night with two of his buddies. A terrible wind came and capsized the boat, and Oliver, my darling, handsome, and powerful Oliver, drowned in the Nantucket Sound.

It's past midnight now, and I'm wide awake, trying not to cry too loudly. Around me, this big house Neal calls "the Remington House" feels like a prison. I thought I was on my way to a brand-new life with a love that I could actually count on.

But instead, Oliver has left me, just as I thought he would. He's left me here, on this earth and in this life, all by myself.

Oh, Oliver. Why. Why. Why.

September 3, 1978

Attending Oliver's funeral was difficult, but I was bent on going. Eventually, I found a babysitter to take over during the afternoon, then dressed in all black and drove myself to the church. Nobody at the service knew me as Oliver's girlfriend, as the woman he'd pledged his life to. Probably, everyone thought I was just there to rubberneck and gossip.

Unfortunately, midway through the service, I broke down, sobbing. I got a few strange looks, and I probably started a bit of gossip of my own.

Because of the nature of his death, they never found his body, which has made things incredibly hard to accept. I still have this sense that he'll appear outside the door one day, smiling at me like he did that first time in his office, as though he knew everything about me.

September 5, 1978

I have returned to the mundanity of my old life. I scarcely know how to get out of bed some days. Besides Carmella and Elsa, I have nothing to live for.

I miss Oliver so incredibly. I might just fall apart.

September 7, 1978

I received a call this afternoon that rocked me to the core. It was Oliver's lawyer, a man named Fred, and he wanted me to come to his office to go over something Oliver had written in his will.

I couldn't get a babysitter, so I packed up Carmella and Elsa and took them downtown, where we waited in the lawyer's lobby to be called in. When I entered, the lawyer laughed at Carmella and Elsa and then smiled nervously at me. It occurred to me that he is the only man on earth who knows the nature of my relationship with Oliver.

But then, he told me what Oliver had left me.

The seaside cottage.

Our home together.

It's now all mine.

I had to sign a few pieces of paper, which assured me

that the seaside cottage was mine and mine alone, not my husband's. Afterward, the lawyer gave me the keys, and I headed out, shaking wildly as I drove all the way to the cottage. Once there, Elsa ran wild through the house and Carmella cooed happily on the floor. But I walked through the halls as though I was a ghost haunting the place.

The house itself looked just as it had on that day when I'd sat there, waiting for him to come home. The same stuff was in the fridge, rotting now. The same bread was on the counter.

And in fact, it's late, later than Neal's set dinner time, and the girls and I are still here. I don't know that I want to go back home— but I know I will. I'm not strong enough to be a single woman alone in this world, especially with two children. I wanted to build a life with Oliver, perhaps in this little house. Now that Oliver is gone, I am left to double down on my old life, with hopes that it will eventually be okay again.

Carmella continued to read, her eyes blurry as she sped through her mother's devastating autumn, all the way to the news that she was pregnant with Colton.

Carmella cried openly as she read about her mother's new pregnancy, which she called "a fresh start" for the Remington Family.

"I don't know what to do about the past, nor about how much it still pains me," Tina wrote. "But I know that this new baby is a beautiful gift. And perhaps, if God brings Neal a little boy, he will find a way to love me again, and we can finally be happy."

Carmella crawled into bed after that, shivering as Cody turned toward her and kissed her on the forehead. In her heart of hearts, she understood Colton's death within the context of her mother's life. She'd thought

Colton had been a fresh start, but instead, he'd been an avenue toward more heartache. Perhaps, Tina had thought Colton's death had been her payment for her affair. She'd stepped out of her marriage, and therefore, she deserved losing a child. It was all too devastating to bear.

"Did you learn how the affair played out?" he asked sleepily.

Carmella sniffed and kissed him again, unsure she wanted to express her mother's trauma aloud. It felt too heavy. Slowly, she and Cody fell into the impossible beauty of sleep, resting for the new dawn— a dawn that Carmella knew she didn't deserve but would love with her full heart, anyway.

Chapter Thirteen

A few minutes before midnight, the door to the room in the bed and breakfast creaked open, and Cole's shadow rushed through the light of the moonlight on the floor. Aria shifted up, watching him as he removed his shirt and changed into a sleeping shirt, his skin flashing like fish beneath the water's surface. When he turned to find Aria watching him, he started, his hand over his chest.

"I'm sorry. I hope I didn't wake you up," Cole said.

Aria's heart thudded. "I didn't think you'd make it back."

Cole frowned and sat at the edge of the bed. "Why not?"

Aria shrugged, remembering the way Julia had looked at him at the bar.

"Did you think I was interested in that woman?" Cole asked, incredulous.

Aria crossed her arms, her cheeks burning with shame. "She was interested in you."

Cole shrugged. "I didn't come to Savannah to pick up

girls."

"Why did you come to Savannah, then?"

Cole dropped back on the bed and placed his hand over the comforter right where Aria's ankle was. The weight of his hand was a comfort. "I came to help you crack the case of the weird letter you received in the mail, remember?"

"It's a long trip for such a stupid reason," Aria said.

Cole gave her a look. "I like going on adventures with you," he added finally. "I thought it would be fun to get away from the Vineyard for a while together. And it has been."

Aria felt the words she wanted to say heavy in her throat. She wanted to ask Cole if he felt what she felt between them. If he thought of her the way she did, endlessly and with a passion that nearly knocked her to her knees.

Instead, she heard herself say, "Yeah. It's been really fun. I mean, you're my best friend."

Cole laughed. "You're my best friend, too."

Aria winced at how small this sounded when compared to the enormity of her feelings.

Cole stuck his hand out, and Aria shook it.

"Best friends for life," Cole said.

"Best friends for life," Aria repeated, feeling the words like a sword through her belly.

Cole raised his head and placed it on his hand, propping himself up with his elbow. "Who do you think sent you that newspaper clipping, anyway? Do you think it was your professor? Judah Heskew?"

Aria frowned, considering this. "He could have just written it in an email."

"Yeah. True."

"Plus, there's the fact that he could have mentioned his friendship with my mother at any time during the three years I was a student here. He never did."

"You should confront him while we're still here," Cole suggested.

Aria's heart twisted with fear. "I don't know..."

"Come on, Aria. Someone sent you that clipping for a reason. You now know more about your mother than you ever did before. And if you're not willing to ask her about her past, maybe you should try the next best thing and ask him."

That night, Cole slept peacefully as Aria stared with terrified eyes through the dark room. Cole's body was only a foot to her left, warm and strong and wonderful, and it took every bit of her strength not to curl up beside him and whisper how much she loved him.

She imagined them years in the future, still calling one another "best friends," as they married other people and even had children. She imagined having to watch Cole be someone else's husband. She imagined befriending this woman and liking her.

Aria would be heartbroken forever if that was her story.

The next morning, Cole woke around seven-thirty. Aria was already wide awake, sipping coffee at the table next to the window and watching Savannah residents stroll to work, their eyes open to a brand new day. Cole smiled sleepily and said, "Did you sleep okay?"

Aria shook her head. "No. But it's okay."

Cole placed his feet on the floor to the side of the bed. "What time do you want to go to the architecture building today?"

"Maybe around eleven," Aria admitted. "Judah

usually starts his office hours, then."

Cole saluted her, then headed to the bathroom. Aria listened as he showered himself, singing a song as the water streamed over him. After he dressed, they headed downstairs to eat breakfast, mostly Southern breakfast dishes slathered in gravy and heavy with potatoes. Aria laughed as they stumbled back out, their bellies full. She felt very slow and happy, and it reminded her of couples she'd seen on campus when she'd been a student, who'd seemed content to wander around, heading no place in particular, as the hours passed. Back then, she hadn't thought she was capable of that kind of love. She'd thought she was doomed to marry someone like Benjamin.

Aria and Cole walked up the grand staircase of the architecture building, then stood in front of Judah's door. Aria took a deep breath, then knocked, half-praying that Judah wasn't there that day, that they couldn't get to the bottom of whatever this was. But then, Judah's familiar, deep voice said, "Come in," and Aria felt herself squeeze the doorknob and twist it.

Aria had spent so many hours in Judah's office in the past. Back in her lonely college years, it had felt like a refuge from the chaos of being a young and lost twenty-something who didn't have any friends. Now, at the threshold yet again, Aria was overwhelmed with the sense that she was returning home.

Judah sat on the other side of his desk, one ankle placed delicately on his knee and a newspaper spread out in front of him. When he lifted his head to look at her, his smile was enormous. He leaped up, his arms opening.

"Aria Baldwin! I can't believe it's you!"

Aria couldn't help it. She laughed, almost giggled

with joy at seeing him, and stepped forward to greet him. Cole was hot on her heels, and he closed the door behind them.

"Hi, Professor," Aria heard herself say.

"So, you got my emails, then? Are you here to re-enroll in courses?" Judah sat back down and smiled at Cole nervously. "And you've brought a friend with you."

"This is Cole," Aria explained. "I met him when I went to the Caribbean last autumn."

"Ah, yes. The trip that took you away from us for good," Judah said, reaching out a hand to shake Cole's. "Although I hated to read about that horrific accident. I hope everyone is all right?"

Aria sat in one of the seats in front of his desk and blushed. "Everyone is okay. It was just an eye-opening experience that required a bit of perspective, if that makes sense."

"It certainly does." Judah frowned. "Where have you been, if I may ask? Getting that perspective, I mean. I can't imagine you returned to Texas."

"No. I've been on Martha's Vineyard," Aria explained.

"Beautiful there," Judah said, clearly confused. "Have you been studying at all? Keeping up to date with news from the architecture world?"

"I haven't had much time. I um. I cut myself off from my father's money, so I've had to work hard to keep myself afloat."

"I imagine so," Judah said with a sigh. "That must have been some trip to the Caribbean. Everything changed for you, it seems."

Aria nodded and laced her fingers together, frightened.

"But if you're here to register for classes this next semester, I have several recommendations for you," Judah went on, "including a class I will be teaching myself."

"I'm not here for that," Aria confessed. "Although I imagine that class will be incredible."

Judah furrowed his brow. "Then, tell me, Aria. What brings you back to Savannah?"

Aria cleared her throat and glanced at Cole, who nodded at her for support. "I was curious about something, Professor. Did you happen to know my mother? Bethany Quinn?"

At this, all the color drained from Judah's face. He placed his hand around his neck and blinked at her, genuinely shocked.

"Where is this coming from?" Judah asked, his voice even lower than normal.

Aria wasn't sure she wanted to get into how she'd learned about this.

"Did your mother tell you that?" Judah asked then, sounding anxious.

Aria tilted her head. "So, you did know her."

Judah stood and placed his hands behind his back. He stuttered and said, "I suppose I have known many people in my life."

Aria rolled her eyes slightly. She felt very quiet and very damaged. "Is that why you always said you liked my work?"

Judah's jaw went slack. "I'm sorry?"

"You always said you thought I was a good architect or that I would be. But did you only say that because my mom was a friend of yours?" Aria asked.

Judah looked flabbergasted.

"The other students knew I was a hack," Aria continued. "They saw right through what I did."

"Aria. Is that why you left?" Judah demanded. "Because the other students said you weren't good enough? Because that's incorrect, Aria. You are an extremely talented architect, and you owe it to yourself to return to this school and graduate."

As Judah spoke, Aria realized he hadn't answered her question and was dancing around it any way he could. There was no way to tell if he lied to her, even now, about her talent or lack thereof.

Slowly, Aria stood and took a step toward the door. Judah's eyes swam with confusion.

"Why don't you want to tell me?" Aria asked, her voice very small. "I spent so many hours in this office, chatting with you about everything in my life. And you never thought to mention this?"

Judah's arms dropped to his sides. He looked defeated. "Aria, there's so much you don't understand," he said.

Aria's heart shattered at his words. She felt just as she had with her own family, that they were unwilling to share themselves with her and get to know her. She felt alone. Before Judah could say another word, she turned on her heel and fled his office. Cole raced after her and remained hot on her heels, even when she broke into a sprint, cutting across campus, her blond hair flowing wildly out behind her. Only when she reached her tree, beneath which she'd spent so many hours in the shade, she faltered, gripped her knees, and let herself cry.

Why wasn't her mother honest with her? And why had Judah kept the past a secret for all these years? None of it meant any sense. And it seemed clearer, every day, that Aria would never get to the bottom of it.

Chapter Fourteen

Carmella watched from the front porch as Aria parked her Chevy in the driveway and walked slowly up to the house. She was tanned from her sailing adventure, and her hair was wild and very blonde from the sun. When she reached the porch, she smiled up at Carmella, then said, "I'm sorry I'm late," as though she was ten minutes late instead of two.

"Honey, you're fine!" Carmella laughed and greeted the young woman with a hug. "Georgia is fast asleep, so you can rest for a little while. She'll need a bottle in about an hour, but that's it."

Aria entered Carmella's house, and Carmella followed after her, dying to ask about her trip to Savannah with Cole. According to Elsa, they'd returned only two days ago, and they remained hush-hush about the state of their relationship. *But how could they have traveled all that way in such close quarters without a single kiss?*

"How was Savannah?" Carmella asked as she put on her shoes.

Aria shrugged. "It was weird to be back."

"Did it make you want to go back to school?"

"I don't know. Not really." Aria grimaced. "It feels like the entire city is filled with ghosts."

Carmella laughed. "Did Cole like it?"

"I think so." Aria bit her lower lip, looking as though she wanted to say something but wasn't sure how. After another pause, she asked, "Do you have big plans today?"

Carmella slid her mother's diary into her bag, her heart hammering. What she was up to today had nothing to do with grocery shopping, seeing a friend, or going to the gym. It felt much more sinister.

"Just a few errands," Carmella said. "Feels like there's never enough time."

Carmella waved goodbye to Aria from her car, then reversed into the road and drove out toward the Remington House. Last night, she'd texted Elsa about their mother's things, about where Elsa kept them, and Elsa explained they were under her bed at the Remington House. Carmella was welcome to go through them when Elsa was at work.

Carmella parked in front of the Remington House and used her key to enter, calling out, "Hello?" Deep within the house, Alyssa's voice hollered back, "Hi!" A moment later, she appeared with a huge smile and a tiny baby bump. "Carmella! What are you doing here?"

Carmella's cheeks burned with embarrassment. *How could she explain her plan?*

"Elsa found a few boxes of our mother's things," Carmella said. "I've been reading her diary from 1977 and 1978, and I was curious if there were any others."

"Oh! Cool. Have you learned any family secrets?" Alyssa asked.

Carmella wanted to sit on the floor with Alyssa and

dig deep into her mother's past, to tell her each of the aching memories Tina had written across the page. But Carmella knew that telling Alyssa these things before Elsa knew was a serious crime. So, she said, "Just a lot of stuff from when I was a baby. It's fascinating to me, at least."

Upstairs, Carmella dropped to the ground beside Elsa's bed and pulled out several of their mother's boxes. One of them was full to the brim with other diaries which spanned other years, both before and after the affair with Oliver, until her death when Carmella had been a teenager.

Carmella removed the diaries from the box, hunted through the corners, and then went through her mother's jewelry box. She then flipped over each box and shook it, listening for some sign of a key clinking.

Where on earth was the key to the sea cottage?

Ever since Carmella had read about it, she'd been hungry to go to this magical place, a home that seemed to be the single greatest solace to Tina during the months after Oliver's death. It sounded like Carmella and Elsa had spent a lot of time there, so much so that Carmella even took her first steps there.

But Carmella didn't remember going to the cottage at all, which meant that Tina had stopped bringing her children there at some point. *Had she continued to go there as Carmella and Elsa had gotten older? Had it remained in her name? Or had something else happened to it after Tina's death?*

Unsure where to turn, Carmella placed her face in her hands and sighed. If the key wasn't in her mother's final collection of possessions, she had no idea where it could be.

Slowly, Carmella began to return Tina's things to the boxes, assembling everything as orderly as possible so as not to annoy Elsa. When she stacked the diaries, she flipped through several of them, noting the day Colton had been born, the day Carmella had started kindergarten, and the day she'd visited Oliver's grave over ten years after his death and told him that she continued to love him. Each of the diary entries was heartbreaking, even in their simplicity, and Carmella found herself sobbing in the light that flooded Elsa's bedroom, overwhelmed with the tragedy of her mother's life.

The final diary was only half-full. Tina had begun it three months before her death, and it recounted plenty of normal days from the lives of Carmella, Elsa, Neal, and Tina back in the nineties. On one page, Tina had written a shopping list, including a Twix, a candy bar Carmella had loved. This very simple detail shattered Carmella.

As Carmella flipped through the diary, it occurred to her that the book itself was a lot heavier than it should have been. She flipped it over to take stock of it, then heard a dramatic clank from within. *Could it be?* Quickly, she flipped through the pages, then discovered a sort of "hole" within the back cover, wherein Tina had placed an ornate key.

Carmella tugged the key from the hole and gazed at it, stunned. This was the only key she'd found within all the possessions, making it her only hope.

Carmella hurried back to her car, waving to Alyssa and Maggie as she went, then started the engine and sped off. According to the hints Tina had written in the diary, Carmella knew almost exactly where the seaside cottage should have been if it still existed. She drove there immediately, hardly able to breathe.

Carmella drove very slowly down the back country road, which had never been paved, peering through the line of budding trees and high weeds. If she wasn't mistaken, it seemed that one area of the road's weeds was slightly shorter, slightly younger, as though, at one point over the past few years, someone had driven through. Too terrified to turn her car down the path, Carmella parked her car on the road, locked it, and dove through the weeds, which attached themselves to her pants and her sweatshirt. A thorn snagged on her arm, and she jumped at the sharp feeling through her skin. She was reminded of one of her favorite books as a child, *The Secret Garden*.

When Carmella reached the line of trees, she grabbed a thick branch and peered over it to find a beautiful stone cottage directly along the water. Because the trees had overgrown in front of the cottage, it couldn't be seen from the water. The trees had cocooned it over the years, as though they'd wanted to reclaim the space.

Carmella pushed herself through the weeds to find a stone trail and then, miraculously, a very cracked and broken driveway. A shiver raced up her spine when she imagined that her mother had once parked her car there, hungry to meet Oliver.

Still, Carmella couldn't be sure that the house was her mother's, not until she tried the key.

At the door nearest the driveway, Carmella removed the key from her pocket and took a deep breath. When she pushed the key through the lock, it entered easily and clicked, but when she tugged at the door to open it, the wood wouldn't budge. The winds, rain, and saltwater had affected the wood over the years, so it now bulged against the doorway. Carmella removed the key from the lock, suddenly very sad. *How could she enter?*

Carmella walked around the side of the cottage to find the front porch that had once looked out over the water. Carmella sat on the stone steps and tried to picture her mother as a young woman with two young daughters, sitting there on the porch and writing in her diary as Oliver cooked for her inside. Tina had thought Oliver was her secret to a better life. *But what if Oliver had taken her away from their family?* Colton never would have been born. Maybe Tina would have had another child, who would have been Carmella's half-sibling. Maybe Tina wouldn't have disliked Carmella so much because Colton never would have died.

Suddenly too overwhelmed to remain on the property a moment more, Carmella jumped up and fled through the weeds and trees back to her car. She started the engine and pressed her foot on the gas, hurrying away from her mother's dark memories. But when she returned to downtown Edgartown, she couldn't just go home. She'd only been gone forty-five minutes and booked Aria for three hours.

More than that, she just couldn't carry this story alone anymore. She had to tell Elsa.

Carmella drove to the Katama Lodge and parked out front. Her hands were clammy, and she struggled to get a full breath. As she entered the front door, the receptionist, Theresa, who'd taken over after Mallory had begun to pursue law greeted her happily and said, "You shouldn't be here! You're not back to work till June." But Carmella waved her hand and said something easy, something Carmella couldn't remember after the fact, that assured her Carmella just "couldn't stay away."

Carmella knocked on Elsa's door and was grateful to hear Elsa's voice on the other side. "Come in!" Carmella opened it to find Elsa and Janine seated together, both with green smoothies.

"Carmella!" Janine and Elsa greeted her in unison.

"What are you doing here?" Janine popped up to hug her, and Elsa did the same.

"Aria's watching Georgia," Carmella explained, her voice jumpy.

"Isn't that nice? Elsa was just telling me she thinks Aria and Cole are in love," Janine said conspiratorially.

"Cole and Aria won't tell me anything," Elsa said. "Maybe you can get something out of Aria?"

Carmella tried to laugh, but it sounded strange. "Do you mind if I talk to you for a minute?"

Janine eyed Elsa curiously, then bowed her head and said, "I'll see you later!"

After Janine disappeared through the door and closed it behind her, Elsa raised an eyebrow and asked, "What's going on, Carm?"

Carmella felt shaky, as though she hadn't eaten enough. She leaned against Elsa's desk and crossed her arms, unable to come up with the right words.

"Carmella? Is Georgia okay?" Elsa looked really worried now.

"Yes. Everyone is fine." Carmella swallowed. "Do you remember the diary you gave me a few months ago? Mom's from when I was a baby?"

Elsa brightened. "Of course! I've been reading over the diary from when I was a baby in parallel. It's so fun to hear about how her and Dad's life was immediately after they married."

Carmella nodded. "I'm sure."

"They just seem so happy and in love," Elsa went on.

"It reminds me of when I was first pregnant with Cole, and Aiden used to dote on me."

Carmella's heart sank. "Elsa. Mom was having an affair."

Immediately, Elsa's face fell. "What are you talking about?"

"After I was born, Mom was depressed. She had to go to therapy for a while, which is how she met Oliver Matthews and eventually fell in love with him," Carmella said, speaking very quickly.

Elsa shook her head. "That's crazy, Carm."

"It's true," Carmella said.

"Why have we never even heard of this guy?" Elsa demanded.

"Oliver died right before Mom got up the nerve to leave Dad," Carmella explained, her voice breaking.

"He died?"

"In a boating accident," Carmella went on. "Mom was devastated. But he left her a seaside cottage in his will. I just went out to see it."

Elsa's mouth hung open with shock.

Carmella removed the key from her pocket and lifted it so that it glinted in the light. Elsa took it and held it, looking at it as though she wanted to hurl it out the window.

"I didn't know how to tell you," Carmella continued.

Elsa remained speechless for a very long time. "I wish you wouldn't have," is what she finally said after a while, her words thick with resentment.

Carmella stared at Elsa, genuinely shocked. "You should come with me to the cottage. It's beautiful. It sounds like Mom went there when she needed quiet time, when she needed to feel like herself. And ever since she died, nobody has been out there."

Elsa couldn't look Carmella in the eye.

"She used to take us there, even," Carmella explained. "I took my first steps there, and you used to run around, playing with your dolls."

"I don't remember that at all," Elsa said stiffly, as though that meant anything.

Carmella wasn't accustomed to Elsa being so cold. She slowly took the key back from Elsa and slid it into her pocket, sensing that she had built a wall between herself and this truth.

"I just can't believe Mom would do that to Dad," Elsa finished, her lips in a paper-thin line.

"Dad wasn't always kind to Mom," Carmella continued quietly. "Apparently, when they had you, they lived a fairy tale life of wedded bliss. But after I came, things were difficult. Dad was consumed with the Katama Lodge, as deep as he could go, and he hardly came out to check if Mom was okay taking care of two little girls alone."

Elsa shook her head again, as though none of Carmella's words could penetrate her mind. Carmella sighed and turned back toward the door.

"Yes, well." Elsa rushed out, hunting for another topic. "Did you get your invitation to the party in June? It's serving as a going-away party for me and a party for both Maggie and Alyssa's babies." She laughed, but the pitch of it was a little too high.

Carmella nodded. "I got the invite. I'll be there."

Elsa made a face that told Carmella she never wanted to hear about Oliver Matthews or the seaside cottage again. Carmella said several more pleasantries, then left the office, feeling as though she'd been slapped. By the time she reached her car, she was crying in honor of the memories of her mother, who'd done anything she could to keep herself afloat in Neal's world of neglect.

Chapter Fifteen

Something had definitely shifted after the trip to Savannah. Aria could sense it in Cole's eyes when they hung out together, talking endlessly about whatever was on their minds deep into the night. Once, Cole's hand had brushed against Aria's on a walk along the pier, and Aria had nearly fallen to her knees. His touch was the most powerful thing she understood.

It was early June, and miraculously, Aria didn't have a shift at the bar or a babysitting gig lined up, and even Cole had cleared his schedule of sailing jobs. Early, they woke and grabbed coffee at a cute coffee shop in Edgartown, where they shared a scone and watched the tourists as they strode through Edgartown like they owned the place. As Aria had already lived on the island for the better part of a year, she felt a deeper sense of understanding of the place, one that allowed her to understand that the heart of Martha's Vineyard went beyond the sunny days. It existed on the coldest, darkest day in February, on the most tumultuous day of hurricane season.

"Do you think you can make it to the party Saturday?" Cole asked, giving Aria a half-smile.

"I can make it," Aria said, her heart jumping. "Should I bring anything?"

"My mom, aunts, and step-grandmother always make too much food to go around," Cole explained. "Just bring yourself."

Aria burned to ask Cole what her role at the party would be. *Was she going as his girlfriend? Or just as his friend?* Oh, but it didn't matter. She was just grateful to be invited at all.

Saturday morning, Aria dressed in a light pink dress and styled her hair and makeup expertly, the way she would have back in Texas. Cole picked her up around eleven and drove her through the sun-dappled island as the radio played oldies. When they pulled up outside the Remington House, six cars already lined the property, and music billowed out from the back porch.

Aria and Cole walked around the side of the house to say hello to the people gathered along the beach and the porch, all in beautiful summer linens and big sunglasses. Alyssa and Maggie, the pregnant sisters, hurried down the porch steps to hug both Aria and Cole as Alyssa exclaimed, "It's the famous Aria! Cole has done his best to hide you away from us."

Aria blushed, grateful for Alyssa's enormous personality. It seemed Alyssa always knew what to say.

"Cole? Why have you been hiding her?" Alyssa demanded.

"Don't mind her," Maggie said with a smile. "Can I get you something to drink? A lemonade? An Aperol Spritz?"

Alyssa followed Maggie onto the porch to select a

drink, where she greeted Mallory, Cole's little sister, who carried her toddler, Zachery, and spoke to Bruce Holland about all things law. Aria introduced herself, feeling the intensity of their gazes.

"We've been so curious about the mystery woman Cole met in the Caribbean!" Mallory said.

"I'm no mystery," Aria said.

After that, Elsa burst from the back door to hug Aria and usher her deeper into the house. She pressed a glass of wine into Aria's hand and introduced her to her step-mother, Nancy, and her stepsister, Janine, who worked as a naturopathic doctor at the Katama Lodge.

"Where's Carmella?" Aria heard herself ask with a smile.

A wave of annoyance passed over Elsa's face. "She's around here somewhere."

Aria stalled with confusion, as she'd thought Carmella and Elsa were above petty fights of siblings.

When Aria returned to the porch, she found Cole with a toddler named Lucy in his arms. Lucy was adorable, babbling to Cole about this and that as Maggie adjusted her dress over her chunky thighs.

"Hello, there," Aria said to the little girl.

"This is Lucy," Maggie explained.

"Oh! Lucy. I've heard all about you," Aria said, remembering the story Cole had told her about Alyssa's ex-boyfriend and the little girl he couldn't care for. "Is Cole taking good care of you?"

"Cole!" Lucy cried, which made everyone laugh.

"She's Cole's number one fan," Maggie explained.

"You jealous?" Cole teased Aria, and Aria's cheeks burned with embarrassment. In truth, all she could think of now was a future Cole holding their child. She couldn't shake the image from her mind for a long time.

Janine's fiancé, Henry, who worked as a documentary filmmaker, was at the grill, asking everyone what kind of burgers they wanted. Aria opted for a veggie burger, which Henry placed on the grill with a smile as Cole passed Lucy back to Maggie. Maggie kissed Lucy on the cheek, then spoke directly to Aria.

"Have you met my boyfriend, David?"

Maggie placed her hand around the bicep of a handsome, bespectacled man beside her with curly and wild hair. According to what Cole had told her, David was a rather new person in Maggie's life, as she was in the midst of getting divorced.

"Hi, David! I'm Aria."

"Hi!" David looked slightly nervous, and he had a small sunburn on his arms. "Are you used to big family parties?"

"No," Aria said. "Well, not ones where everyone is nice, anyway."

David laughed.

"You're a writer, aren't you?" Aria remembered.

"Yes," David said. "I met Maggie when she came to the city to convince me to visit my mother here in the Vineyard."

"Quite a story," Aria said.

"My mother sure thinks so," David joked. "She's around here somewhere, telling everyone just how happy she is to be a grandmother."

David pointed out his mother, Heidi, who sat with Carmella and Cody on the other side of the porch. As they chatted, Carmella raised a hand to wave to Aria, and

Aria waved back. It felt miraculous to be a part of such a tremendous family.

"How long have you and Cole been together?" David asked.

"Oh! Um. We're not really, um." Aria shrugged.

"Okay. I'm sorry if I overstepped," David said with a smile.

"Hey!" Cole appeared beside Aria with a plate upon which he'd already put together her veggie burger, remembering all the toppings and condiments she liked.

"Wow," Aria said. "You even remembered how much I love pickles!"

"I would never forget something so weird," Cole said.

"Cole? Yours is ready, too!" Henry called, and Cole disappeared for a moment to prep his burger. As Aria waited, she scanned the porch, taking in the vision of so many people coming together to celebrate the new babies, Elsa's move with Bruce Holland, and the first day of summer, which was just in a little more than a week. For the first time in a while, Aria considered what her family was up to, whether or not they'd had any family dinners lately, and how big Roger had gotten since she'd last seen him.

Cole and Aria grabbed seats on the porch to eat their burgers as they watched the waves roll onto the beach. Elsa and Bruce sat near them and squabbled gently about what color to paint the downstairs bathroom of their new place, which made Cole lean down to Aria's ear and whisper, "It makes me happy to hear my mom have such normal arguments with Bruce. After my dad died, I wasn't sure she would ever find a way to be normal again, you know?"

Aria nodded, her heart ballooning at Cole's tremendous love for his family.

Not long after Aria ate, Cole went inside to chat with some of the men in the family, and Aria remained on the porch with her lemonade. Carmella spotted her and beelined for her, greeting her with a squeeze to the elbow.

"How are you doing? I hope the party isn't too overwhelming."

Aria shook her head. "It's lovely. Is baby Georgia around here somewhere?"

"She's asleep upstairs," Carmella said, showing off the baby monitor in her left hand.

"She's such a sweetie," Aria said, remembering the gentle and lovely way Georgia kicked her feet and smiled up at Aria.

"Yes." Carmella eyed Elsa, who passed them by without saying hello. As Elsa gathered several glasses, Janine and Nancy followed her inside, and Aria and Carmella were suddenly the only people on the porch.

Suddenly, Carmella's tone dropped an octave. "Elsa is very upset right now."

Aria was surprised Carmella wanted to be so open. "I noticed something was off."

Carmella winced. "She thinks I'm digging around in family business that is better left alone."

Aria was intrigued. "I've sort of been doing the same thing."

"Yeah?" Carmella cocked her head. "Did you learn anything devastating?"

"I don't know," Aria admitted, thinking of her mom at Savannah College of Art and Design. "I don't have the full story yet."

"I do," Carmella explained. "And Elsa refuses to accept it."

"What is it?" Aria asked. "If you don't mind telling."

"I feel overwhelmed with it, actually," Carmella said, "so it would be nice to talk about it."

"Go ahead."

Carmella took a deep breath, then proceeded to tell Aria her mother's story. She told her about the affair her mother had had with Oliver Matthews, then her father's neglect of the marriage and Oliver's death, and about the will that had left the sea cottage to Tina so many years ago.

"I went to the cottage," Carmella continued. "It's still there and still gorgeous. But I couldn't get in. The door wood is swollen and bulging into the sides."

Aria shook her head. "It probably needs a lot of work."

Carmella nodded. "I'm assuming so."

Aria sat quietly, spinning with an idea that she felt slightly too terrified to say aloud. But before she could brush the thought away, Carmella caught on.

"Wait a minute. Aren't you an architect?"

"Not yet," Aria said with a laugh.

"Yes, but you did three years at architecture school," Carmella pointed out.

"I did."

Carmella brightened. "Maybe you could come with me to the house?"

Aria's heartbeat escalated. The seaside cottage spoke to her most romantic fantasies. "I can't promise I'll know how to fix it."

"To be honest with you, I need moral support to go back there," Carmella said under her breath. "Elsa's reaction was a bit devastating."

"I'd be happy to go with you," Aria affirmed, smiling. "Let's go to your mother's cottage and break down the door!"

Carmella laughed. "It feels like we're breaking down the door to my mother's past."

Aria nodded, thinking that she, too, had recently done that on her quest to Savannah. But after her trip, the trail had fizzled out. Judah Heskew seemed unwilling to talk about her mother at all, and it remained unclear who had sent her that newspaper clipping.

Still, it would feel good to sink her teeth into another mystery from the past. This one was easier because it didn't belong to her at all.

Chapter Sixteen

The next week, Carmella picked Aria up outside her apartment building and drove her out to the stone seaside cottage along the water. Aria trampled through the weeds and between the trees to reach the gorgeous little place, then watched as Carmella slid the key into the back door and shrugged after she tried to shove it open. Aria then remembered a trick she'd learned once, wherein she used a stick as a sort of lever to pulse open the door without actually breaking it. Very quickly, they were in.

"You're a genius," Carmella breathed, walking through the door for the first time as Aria followed her, her heart in her throat.

Just as Carmella had said, nobody had been at the cottage since Tina's death, when Carmella herself had been a teenager. The nearby sea had taken its toll on the old place, and a few windows had been broken, allowing various animals to find a home within the walls. Debris was cluttered throughout, alongside what was left of what Tina and Oliver had positioned with purpose: chairs, couches, and a very old television that clearly no longer worked. In the kitchen stood an old cabinet where Oliver or Tina had housed beautiful china.

"It's like walking back through time," Aria breathed as she walked gingerly through the clutter.

Aria and Carmella shoved open the door to the porch to air out the old house, then set to work on a list of things to do to get the place back in shape. The first thing was obvious: the interior needed to be cleaned, and the old wood needed to be removed. Probably, a handyman needed to be hired to take out the entire back porch and build a new one.

"All in good time," Carmella said excitedly.

Aria laughed, genuinely pleased with the old place. She pointed out from the porch at the beach and said, "We need to clear some of those trees, as well. This could be a spectacular view, but it's all boxed in."

Carmella nodded. "Write down 'call a tree guy.'"

Aria did so, amazed at the length of the list already. "I'm going to ask Cole to come over to help me clear some of the debris," she said.

"Oh, honey. You don't have to do that."

"We want to," Aria said, her heart lifting. She liked nothing more than spending long, easy hours with Cole, working toward something together. That's what it had been like out on the boat as they'd sailed down to Savannah, and she'd prayed those days would last forever.

Not long afterward, Carmella had to head home to care for Georgia so Cody could return to work. Cole was already on his way, so Aria remained on the porch that was meant to overlook the water, her ears craning for the first sign of Cole's car.

"Hello?" Cole's voice bounced through the old

cottage as he entered, and Aria burst to her feet to greet him. Through the shadows, Cole emerged, his smile enormous. "Is this place even real?"

Aria laughed and hurried through the living room, careful not to trip on anything, before she reached him and hugged him. It was rare that she listened to her body's needs like that and allowed herself such seamless pleasure. Their hug went on a little too long before they broke it and smiled at one another.

They got started, unafraid to get their hands dirty. Bit by bit, they cleared the debris from the living room, the bedroom, and the kitchen, listening to the speaker Cole had brought that played their favorite songs. Very soon, Aria worked up a sweat, then watched as Cole worked easily, his shirt wet with sweat.

After three hours of hard work, Aria and Cole sat on the back porch with two cans of beer and leaned against the house's stone wall, listening to the water. A huge pile of trash and debris sat on the other side of the house, which they would only add to tomorrow.

"I can't believe this place," Cole admitted, then sipped his beer.

Aria nodded. "This woman had this whole entire life and this whole entire affair, all before you were ever born."

"She died, too," Cole reminded her. "And my entire life, all anybody ever said about her was how kind and good she was. Well, that's how my mom talks about her, at least."

"Carmella mentioned Elsa isn't too happy about the cottage."

Cole grimaced. "I didn't tell her I was coming over to help clean it out."

Aria placed her head on Cole's shoulder. Why did it seem easier, sometimes, to keep secrets from those you loved?

"This place will be something special by the end of the summer," Aria affirmed. "I can just imagine it."

"You think Carmella and Cody will want to move out here?"

"I don't know!" Aria smiled, imagining little Georgia running along the porch in a few years' time. "It was her mother's refuge. Maybe it could serve as that for Carmella, as well."

"Then again, Carmella doesn't have anything to run away from," Cole reminded her.

"I guess we don't know that," Aria pointed out. "Every woman needs a few secrets and a place to be herself completely."

"Do you have secrets, Aria Baldwin?"

"What a silly question. I have plenty." Aria shoved him gently with her elbow as Cole laughed.

Cole and Aria sat quietly for a moment, as though they both stirred in stories they couldn't possibly say aloud. Aria burned with desire to kiss him, then watched the moment pass by again.

"I have a question," Cole said.

"Okay. Ask away."

"Have you spoken to your mother at all about what we learned in Savannah?"

Aria shook her head. "No."

"I'm sure she would love to hear from you, even if it was about that."

Bethany Baldwin's face flashed through Aria's mind. In the image, she smiled gently at Aria before turning back to face her father, Kenny. She was always in support of Kenny. Always, Kenny came first.

"Whoever my mother was back in the nineties, she doesn't exist anymore," Aria said simply. "Bethany Baldwin is now exclusively the wife of Kenny Baldwin and the mother of Natalie and Gregory. She has no time for beautiful things like art, design, or silly seaside cottages filled with secrets."

"How do you know that?" Cole asked.

Aria stood and brushed herself off, eyeing the debris that remained in the house. More than anything, she wanted to escape this conversation.

"Let's keep working for a little while and then grab a pizza," she suggested. "I'll buy."

Cole followed Aria back into the cottage, wordless. As Aria continued to work, she felt his eyes burning into her, as though he struggled not to say something that was heavy on his mind. But before he could, Aria turned on the music and played one of his favorite songs, which he began singing along to, almost without thought.

Chapter Seventeen

The Remington family was always there for one another, no matter the season. Even though Carmella and Elsa were still barely speaking, Carmella put on a pair of shorts and a tank top and met Elsa and the rest of her family at the Remington House. It was a sweltering day in June to move the last of Elsa's things down to her new place with Bruce, but it had to be done.

Elsa was a mess, to say the least. As Carmella entered, she threw herself forward to hug her, saying, "It feels almost as hard as when I moved out to live with Aiden so many years ago. So much has changed, but so much has also stayed the same."

Carmella laughed as Bruce entered the room, smiling at Elsa, who was heavy with tears.

"I told her she doesn't have to move in with me," Bruce said. "We just had all those builders come and create the very best and dreamiest house we could have ever imagined, but if she wants to stay here in her childhood bedroom, that's fine with me."

Elsa swatted Bruce playfully and sniffed at Carmella as Janine, Henry, Mallory, Mallory's boyfriend, and David entered to carry boxes and furniture. As they went out, one after another, Carmella was reminded of last year when someone robbed the Remington House to get back at Aiden, a man who'd died and didn't care about belongings anymore.

Carmella carried a box of books to Bruce's truck, positioning them next to a big bookshelf and a box marked "clothes." As she turned back to retrieve more items, Bruce stopped her and spoke under his breath. "Elsa has been so broken up about this situation with your mom."

Carmella's stomach twisted. "I wanted to tell her the truth."

Bruce nodded. "She knows that. And she's working hard to accept it. I just wanted you to know that."

Carmella's throat was thick with tears. She hurried past Bruce to grab another box, then followed after Henry and Janine as they piled a bedside table onto the truck. Very soon, everything Elsa wanted to bring was secured back there, and Bruce and Elsa piled into the front and waved.

"Everyone! Barbecue at our house in an hour," Bruce announced. "I have beer, wine, and enough chicken to go around. Bring anything else you might want. Let's christen this place!"

Carmella texted Cody about the spontaneous family party, and he wrote back that he'd bring Georgia and Gretchen very soon. Afterward, Carmella, Nancy, Janine, and Mallory collapsed in the kitchen to drink water, listening to the house as it creaked and groaned around them.

Recently, Mallory had moved in with her boyfriend,

who'd taken on the role of "stepfather" of Zachery fluidly. Mallory and her boyfriend were adorable, holding hands when they could and speaking as though nobody else in the world existed.

Carmella met Cody, Georgia, and Gretchen down at Elsa's new house, which was half the size of the Remington House, perfect for a couple in their forties prepared for the second half of their lives. Elsa greeted them joyfully. She'd changed into a beautiful blue summer dress and walked them through the house, pointing out the tiles in the bathroom and the cabinets she liked in the kitchen. When they reached the back veranda, Bruce was at the barbecue, already flipping chicken like his life depended on it.

"It looks like you two already belong here," Cody said.

Elsa laughed as she set the outdoor table, her eyes alight. A moment later, Cole appeared on the back porch, smiling at his mother. "All the boxes are in your bedroom," he explained as he cracked a beer.

"Thank you for doing that," Elsa said. "Carmella, if you ever need someone strong to lift stuff around your house, Cole's your guy."

Carmella blushed, remembering that Cole had spent a great deal of the past week at the seaside cottage, clearing debris and clutter with Aria. Cole sipped his beer, giving Carmella a funny look, saying nothing.

Everyone else arrived in groups: Janine and Henry, Nancy, Mallory, her boyfriend and her son, Maggie, David, and Alyssa. Carmella put Georgia down for a nap and sat out on the back porch, where the air sizzled with expectation. There was something about the first night at a new place— something that set the stage for the rest of the time there.

"I think we should make a toast," Nancy said, raising her glass of wine. "To Elsa and Bruce and their amazing new chapter."

Everyone else followed suit, raising their glasses so that they reflected the orange and pink glint of the sunset. Elsa blushed and kissed Bruce gently, her engagement ring displayed prominently as she squeezed his bicep.

Not long after that, Bruce's partner at the law office, Susan Sheridan Frampton, arrived with her husband, Scott. They'd brought a bottle of wine and a beautiful plant as a housewarming present, and they smiled and greeted everyone as they sat at the picnic table. Carmella was in awe of women like Susan, who were so driven and business-oriented yet also seemed to balance their family's needs with their needs. *How did she do it?*

As Susan, Bruce, and Mallory discussed the Sheridan Law Office, Elsa squeezed Carmella's arm and tilted her head toward the house. "Can I show you something?"

Carmella hadn't seen such kindness in Elsa's eyes since before she'd told Elsa about Tina's affair. Carmella nodded and followed Elsa into the house, then up the stairs to the bedroom Elsa planned to share with Bruce, where Cole had created a mountain of boxes.

"It's this one, I think," Elsa muttered to herself as she slid a massive box onto the bed and opened it. Within were stacks of their mother's diaries. Carmella's heart thudded with fear.

Elsa withdrew a thick, old-fashioned photo album, which she placed delicately on the mattress. She then turned to Carmella to say, "I'm sorry about how I reacted when you told me about Oliver. I didn't want to believe that Mom and Dad's love wasn't the very best love ever. But if I'm honest with myself, what 'love' isn't complicated? So long after his death, I told myself that Aiden was the perfect husband and father, and in many ways, he was. But if I let myself, I can remember the ways he frustrated me. I can remember a time or two when I thought he flirted with someone else. We were married for decades, and I believe we were always faithful to one another. But marriage is complicated. I should recognize that, especially because I'm entering into a new marriage myself."

Elsa opened the photo album and removed several photographs of Elsa and Carmella at various ages. Beneath those photographs, Tina had hidden some, placing them behind the "easy" photographs as a way to hide her affair from Neal.

There were ten photographs with Oliver in them. Carmella was breathless, trying to take in every detail. In one photograph, Tina and Oliver were seated on the front porch of the seaside cottage, and Oliver had his arm slung around Tina's shoulder. Their smiles were enormous, glorious— proof of a happiness that seemed to transcend time and space.

In two, Tina had photographed Oliver with her daughters. In one, Oliver held baby Carmella as Elsa wrapped her arms around one of his legs. He was laughing as though Elsa had just said something adorable. Had anyone else seen the photograph, they'd have assumed he was their father.

"I sobbed and sobbed when I found them," Elsa explained softly.

"How did you?" Carmella asked, flabbergasted.

Elsa shrugged. "I was going through this photo album when I was supposed to be packing. I was looking at photos of Dad and Mom during that time you said the affair happened, and I couldn't help but notice their faces are shadowed. They don't stand near one another in photographs. They seem at a great distance from one another."

Carmella nodded as Elsa flipped through the book, showing this difficult time of Tina and Neal's marriage.

"I don't know what to do about Mom's love for this man," Elsa said. "But because I want to keep loving my mother, and because I love knowing more about my mother, all I can do is love their love."

Carmella sat at the edge of the bed, her chest heavy. "When we were kids, Mom and Dad seemed pretty in love. Don't you think?"

"I remember they held hands a lot," Elsa said. "And laughed."

"I haven't gotten that far in the diaries," Carmella said. "I don't know how Mom found a way back to loving Dad. But isn't it amazing that it happened?"

Elsa wiped a tear from her cheek. "If what you said about him is true, I don't know if he deserved her love."

"He did," Carmella said, although she wasn't entirely sure what it meant to "deserve" love. "He loved us in his own way. And later, he became the kind of father we needed."

"Not when it came to Karen," Elsa said, remembering their stepmother.

"He got out of that when he could," Carmella reminded her. "I didn't tell you any of this to demonize Dad, anyway. I just told you..."

"Because it's a great story," Elsa sighed. "And now that I've sat with it for a while, I'm so glad I have it." She paused, then lifted the photograph, wherein she clung hard to Oliver's leg. "I must have really cared for him. I must have seen how happy he made Mom."

Carmella leaned forward and wrapped her sister in a hug, her head spinning. Downstairs, someone opened the door to the back porch, and laughter and conversation poured into the big, empty house.

"We can go to the cottage together if you want to," Carmella breathed.

Elsa shook her head. "I don't know that I need to see it. I'm just really glad she had it at the time. She was on a quest for happiness, just like all of us."

Chapter Eighteen

Every July on Martha's Vineyard, islanders opened their arms to the celebration of the summer: the Around the Island Regatta, which brought in hundreds of sailors from all over the world to race around Martha's Vineyard. As this was Aria's first summer on Martha's Vineyard, she was overwhelmed as the population of the island quadrupled in size. Most staggering, of course, was the bar's sudden business, which presented her with hour after hour of back-breaking work deep into the night. The best of it was that the sailors who'd come to the island liked to tip big. Still, during the days leading up to the big race, Aria slept long and hard, only managing to get up, brush her teeth, wash her hair, and speed off to the bar again.

The race itself was held on the Saturday after the Fourth of July. Aria was scheduled to work the lunch rush, which happened to coincide with the race itself, which devastated her. This was Cole's first big race of the season, and she wanted to stand at the edge of the dock and scream his name until he came in.

"You're going to come in first," Aria said as she set up the bar that morning, smiling at Cole.

"I don't know. Tommy Gasbarro is a killer sailor," Cole said, speaking of another man on the island who'd sailed extensively.

"Is that the guy who got hurt a few years back?"

"Yes," Cole said. "But that was a fluke. Every sailor has a fluke now and again."

Suddenly, as though they'd called her with their talk of sailing accidents, Whitney Silverton marched into the bar. Impossibly, she was even tanner and more beautiful than she'd been in May, and she called both of their names excitedly.

"You're going down today, Cole Steel," Whitney said as she hugged him. "And Aria! Goodness, you're still behind the bar at this silly place?"

Aria waved her hand. "It isn't so bad. I just wish I could watch the entire race."

"To tell you the truth, a sailing race is pretty boring to watch from shore," Whitney said. "But if you're working lunch, I guess you'll be out of work to party with us along the docks later?"

"I wouldn't miss it," Aria said, glancing at Cole, whose cheeks were beet red.

At eleven-thirty, from the bar's porch, Aria watched with other bar revelers as the first of the sailors embarked on their mission around the island. The islanders and tourists who'd come to see them off screamed and cried from the docks, reminiscent of those who'd watched the whalers leaving Martha's Vineyard hundreds of years ago. Aria placed her hands around her mouth and hollered, "GO, COLE!" Several other bar dwellers followed her lead, calling Cole's name, as he was a regular and a beloved sailor, especially because he was the son of Aiden.

The race was set to take a couple of hours, and Aria worked herself into a frenzy throughout as a way not to worry about Cole. It was strange to feel so tied up in another person's joy and another person's worries, but she also found it exhilarating, as though it gave her life a gravity.

"The reports are saying Cole's at least in the top ten right now!" One of the regulars, Steve, popped his head over the bar counter to talk to Aria as she changed a keg.

"Top ten?" Aria raised her chin to look at him. "Gosh, can you imagine if Cole gets tenth place? He won't talk to anyone for a week!"

Steve laughed appreciatively as Aria clamped the keg in place and began to pour the first beer. When she always replaced it, the froth was overwhelming, and she had to fill several glasses before she got the perfect pour. As she worked, she laughed at her thoughts, remembering a version of herself who'd never have imagined she would work at a bar, not in a million years.

A little while later, Steve announced that Cole was as high as the top five, although they still had about a half-hour left of the race.

"I might fall apart, Steve," Aria said. "I just might fall to the ground!"

Steve laughed. "Cole's lucky to have a girlfriend like you who cares so much."

Aria's eyes widened, but she didn't correct him. This was the first time anyone had ever referred to Aria as Cole's girlfriend, as though it was old news.

Just before the sailors came in, Steve ordered that

Aria leave the bar and run down to welcome Cole to the finish line.

"There are so many people here who need beers, Steve!" Aria said.

But Steve waved his hand. "You need to get down there. I can pour the beers."

Although it was illegal to allow someone without an alcohol license to take over the bar, Aria had a hunch nobody was paying attention on such a festive day, and Steven could be trusted. She burst from the door, raced along the boardwalk, and headed back to the finish line. As she neared the crowd, she could see Cole's sailboat blasting alongside another one she didn't recognize. When she reached the edge of the dock, she screamed, "COME ON, COLE!" But she knew he couldn't possibly hear her over the whipping winds.

"Aria! Hey!"

Aria turned at the sound of her voice to see Elsa, Carmella, Mallory, Maggie, and Alyssa beside her, waving both at Aria and the ocean before them. Aria laughed and pointed out, saying, "He's so close!"

"He really is!" Maggie said this mostly to Lucy, who she held in her arms.

As the boats grew nearer and nearer, the crowd's roar became like a monstrous hum. More and more, Aria felt sure Cole would cross the finish line first. But at the last second, another one raced ahead of him, and the boats were called, one after another, with Cole in second and Whitney in fourth.

"Second!" Elsa cried, her hand in a fist. "So close!"

But already, Maggie and Alyssa hugged Aria excitedly as Carmella and Elsa cried Cole's name.

"Go get him, Aria!" Alyssa said knowingly, patting her on the shoulder.

Aria raced forward, as though Cole was a magnet, and she could do nothing but go to him. He was tying up his boat along the dock, chatting joyously to the man who'd beaten him. The man had black hair and wide shoulders, and just as he said something to Cole, a beautiful woman with long brunette hair leaped into his boat and screamed, "Tommy Gasbarro! You've done it again!"

Before Cole could step off the boat, Aria decided to follow the lead of Tommy's girlfriend or wife, leaping onto the sailboat to wrap her arms around Cole. Cole cried out, lifting her in a circle as Aria screeched joyfully.

After Cole and Aria clambered out of the boat, Tommy Gasbarro eyed Aria and said, "Your boyfriend is a killer sailor. I guess you already know that."

Aria blushed and eyed Cole, preparing for him to correct Tommy. When he didn't, Aria stuck out her hand and said, "I'm Aria. You were brilliant out there today. Congratulations."

Tommy shook it, his salty curls shaking. "Thank you. This is Lola, by the way."

Lola smiled brightly and took Aria's hand. "I see you understand what being with a sailor is like. They give everything to the sea."

"Almost everything," Aria agreed.

As Lola and Tommy walked hand-in-hand, Aria turned to meet Cole's gaze. "You were incredible."

"I thought you had to be at the bar?" Cole said with a laugh.

Aria jumped up, remembering she'd left Steve there by himself. "I have to get back!"

Cole cackled and grabbed her hand, and together,

they sped off to save Steve from the barrage of sailors coming to get their drinks. At the entrance, Aria said goodbye to Cole and forced her way through the crowd, where she found Steve sweating, manic.

"I'm sorry! I'm sorry!" Aria said as she scurried to pour a pint.

"You saw your man get second?" Steve asked with a wink.

"I did," Aria confirmed, placing a pint on the table and taking a wad of cash. "It was incredible. Thank you for that gift."

Steve shrugged and continued to pour, helping Aria get through the mad rush that stretched on and on, through that hour and into the next, until Aria was finally allowed to leave for the day. Steve ducked under the bar as two other employees from the bar began to fill the space that Aria and Steve had left, then lifted his hand to high-five Aria.

"What a day. We did our own race right here at the bar."

"That's right," Aria said, smiling before she walked out of the crowd and back into the splendorous sun to find Cole.

Overwhelmed with adrenaline, Aria sprinted through the celebratory crowd, everyone with drinks in hand, their eyes alight as the sun burned down upon them. Aria headed for where Cole had tied up his boat, where he found Whitney and her boyfriend, Rowan, with beers, their feet slung over the side of the dock.

"Aria! Hey!" Whitney waved.

"Great job today," Aria said. "Have you seen Cole?"

"He was just here. I think he went to get more

drinks," Whitney explained. "He's been eager for you to get off of work, you know."

Aria blushed and turned, her eyes scanning the crowd for some sign of him. For some reason, she felt really anxious and just wanted to be beside him and tell him again and again how brilliant he was.

Aria pushed through the crowd, then met Elsa and Carmella again, both of whom held glasses of wine.

"Hi, Aria! I bet you're over the moon."

"I am," Aria said. "Have you seen Cole?"

"We just saw him about five minutes ago," Elsa said. "He's been making the rounds, from friend group to friend group to family."

"The race never ends," Aria joked as she hurried off, intent on finding him.

Aria stepped from the mass of the crowd, crossing her arms as she surveyed the back of it. Because so many people were at the party, her cell service was finicky, and Cole wasn't answering his phone. For some reason, she felt as though he was now looking for her, too, as though he'd run into both Whitney and his mother, who'd said she was somewhere out there.

Aria took a deep breath and returned to the crowd with her eyes peeled for him. She pushed herself down the boardwalk, listening to conversations about the race, Whitney Silverton's big return to the world of sailing after "that incident," and Cole Steel's assured future in sailing. Still, she couldn't find him.

When Aria returned to Cole's boat, Whitney and Rowan were gone. Aria sighed and crossed her arms, set on waiting there for Cole until he returned. But when she lifted her eyes to the horizon, she saw someone familiar walking toward her. For a moment, her heart stopped beating.

There, wearing a beautiful two-piece linen summer outfit, her long hair styled beautifully, and her makeup without a single color out of place, was Bethany Baldwin. And she looked at Aria with big eyes, filled with emotion, as though she'd been out in the world, hunting for her, just as Aria had been hunting for Cole.

Chapter Nineteen

Aria couldn't believe it. Her mother, Bethany Baldwin, was in her single-room apartment, her hands wrapped around a mug of tea and her eyes flitting about, taking stock of how little the place was. Surprisingly, Bethany hadn't said a single thing, not since they'd walked in together after the drive from the dock. The Bethany that Aria had always known would have already pointed out the wear and tear of the floorboards. She would have asked how Aria could have possibly fallen asleep on such cheap bedsheets.

Back at the dock, Bethany had spoken very quietly to say, "Can we go someplace to talk?" And Aria had been so stricken at the sight of her, there in the place she'd run to hide from her family, that she'd guided her back to her Chevy and driven them back here.

"Is the tea okay?" Aria asked nervously, still standing.

Bethany nodded. "It's wonderful." Aria was pretty sure she hadn't taken a sip yet.

Aria's phone buzzed in her pocket, and she removed it

to find that Cole had called her four times in the past ten minutes. *How hadn't she felt the vibrations?*

"Hey," she answered, turning away from her mother so that she faced the fridge.

"Hey! Whitney said she just saw you. You ran off somewhere?"

Aria's throat was tight with confusion. "I had to go home."

Cole's voice dimmed. "Oh. Is there something wrong? Are you sick?"

"I'm not sick," Aria explained. "I'll call you later, okay? I can't talk now."

"Um? Okay?" Cole sounded flabbergasted, as though he wanted to demand why Aria was suddenly giving him such mixed signals. Finally, they seemed on the path to some kind of romance. She didn't want to make it seem like she was pulling away. *How could she assure him that all she wanted in the world was him? How could she explain that she wanted to be wrapped in his arms as the sailing party erupted around them?*

"I love you, Cole," Aria said spontaneously, surprising herself. And before he could answer back, she hung up, gasping quietly.

Behind her, Bethany echoed the word, "Love?"

Aria turned to blink down at her mother, who looked weak and imperfect, so unlike her normal persona.

"Why are you here, Mom?" Aria asked, silencing her phone.

Bethany deigned to sip the tea, which made her wrinkle her nose. "I got a call yesterday about you."

"What do you mean?"

Bethany sighed and placed the mug of tea on the

bedside table without a coaster, which would have been grounds for prison back in the house she'd raised Aria in.

"Professor Judah Heskew," Bethany said finally. "He said you were on campus recently, asking him questions about me."

Aria studied her mother for a long moment of silence, waiting for her to say something else. When she didn't, Aria retrieved the newspaper clipping from the counter, which she handed over to her mother. For a long time, Bethany studied the image, her lips round.

"Where did you get this?" Bethany asked.

Aria shrugged. "Someone mailed it to me."

"You're kidding."

"Why would I kid about that? The better question is, why wouldn't you tell me that you went to Savannah College of Art and Design?" Aria demanded. "And why wouldn't you tell me that you knew Professor Heskew? I swear, I must have mentioned him to you hundreds of times."

"You haven't said much to me over the past few years, let alone mentioned Judah's name," her mother said.

Aria's eyes widened. Never in her life had she assumed Bethany Baldwin was capable of feeling hurt by something Aria had done.

"I remember the first time you mentioned wanting to go to the Savannah College of Art and Design," Bethany said, her eyes still on the newspaper clipping. "I had just received mail meant for alumni, along with a magazine that included photographs of the various artwork and architecture alumni had made over the years. Gosh, I felt so ashamed looking at that magazine. I remembered having a unique talent and realized I'd wasted it.

"I meant to recycle the magazine. But somehow, you

got a hold of it. I caught you flipping through it in the living room, trying to talk to Natalie about your opinions on architecture. Obviously, you didn't know very much back then, but you sounded like you had good instincts. It took everything within me not to correct you or try to have a conversation about it."

Aria stuttered. "Why didn't you? I would have loved that."

"You wouldn't have," Bethany corrected. "You were nineteen, and you thought I was a representation of all things stupid and evil. Besides, I suppose you don't remember, but I told you that there were other architecture schools—better ones, which made you dig your heels in more. You wouldn't consider applying anywhere else but Savannah." Bethany laughed softly and wiped a tear from your cheek. "And then, I got really excited, you know? Because I felt like you could redo my life for me. That you could go back and undo all of my mistakes."

Aria gaped at her mother, stirring with confusion. Bethany Baldwin thought she'd made mistakes?

"But then came the kicker. You told your father and I that you didn't want help moving to Savannah, that you wanted to do a lot of it on your own. Your father was pretty proud of that, but it broke my heart. I'd begun to dream of returning to that campus, of reliving my past. But before I could find a way to explain my background in architecture, you were already on your way there. And before I knew it, you were thriving."

Aria pressed her lips together, genuinely at a loss. Her confusion only mounted when Bethany began to sob.

"Mom!" Aria hurried to the bed and sat next to her mother, whom she'd hardly hugged in years. The distance between their souls seemed almost insurmountable. Yet here she sat in Aria's small apartment.

"I'm sorry." Bethany shook her head and placed the newspaper clipping to the side.

"It's okay," Aria stuttered. When Bethany's sobbing slowed, she asked, "So you're still friends with Judah?"

Bethany closed her eyes. "Not exactly."

"But he still reached out to you to tell you I'd been on campus recently?" Aria asked.

Bethany opened her eyes again to stare directly into Arias. "Judah was my college boyfriend and my very first love."

Aria's jaw dropped as Bethany nodded. Color returned to her cheeks, as though she'd just unburdened herself from a horrific weight.

"All this time?" Aria stuttered. "Why didn't he ever tell me he knew you?"

"Oh gosh. It's all so complicated." Bethany rubbed her temples.

"Why?" Aria felt they were spinning in circles. "And why did you and Judah break up in the first place?"

"Judah took a fantastic internship after our senior year and left the United States for a while," Bethany explained. "I was heartbroken, but I was also sassy— and I wanted to prove to him that I could do my own thing, too. I moved to Texas and began working as an intern at a pretty good firm. Around that time, I met your father. He was handsome and arrogant and very, very rich. He surprised me with a trip to the Bahamas, then a trip to Alaska, then a trip to Paris. It seemed that every day with him was an adventure of sorts just because of the freedom that money allowed us.

"I can see the way you're looking at me now," Bethany

went on. "Your eyes are judgmental. You can't understand why I would abandon someone cool and smart like Judah for someone like your father."

"I wasn't thinking that," Aria said, although she had been. *Had her mother been able to read her mind for the past twenty-four years?*

"It's okay," Bethany offered. "Your father didn't transform into the man you know, into this cruel and manipulative person, until a little after Gregory was born. It took me a little longer to lose the baby weight, and I struggled with undiagnosed depression. Neither of those things fit well with Kenny's image of how his life should be.

"Not long after that, we had Natalie, and things seemed to only worsen," Bethany continued. "I'd lost the baby weight quicker this time, thank goodness— but I'd also begun dreaming about architecture again. When I told Kenny I was thinking about returning to work, he insinuated it would be impossible since I'd so easily dropped my career after marrying him. He said, basically, who would want me at my age without any real experience?"

Aria's jaw dropped, although she wasn't fully surprised. This was Kenny Baldwin to a T.

Bethany stared at the ground. "The phone call from Judah came out of the blue, honestly. I'd thought of him endlessly and kept up with his career as best as I could. But I hadn't assumed he'd even thought of me since he'd left for Europe.

"On the phone, he told me that he was coming to Texas for a conference soon. Did I want to have dinner? Gosh, the sound of his voice was like drinking water in a desert. I realized that so much of my heart still loved him. I could barely get out of my bed the next day due to fear.

But when he came to town, I arranged for a babysitter for Gregory and Natalie, dressed myself to the nines, and then drove out to meet Judah at a restaurant near his hotel."

"What was Dad doing that night?" Aria asked.

Bethany waved her hand. "He had something to do, a function where they needed to see his face. Whatever it was, it left me in the clear.

"When I arrived at the restaurant, Judah was seated in the corner, wearing a gray suit jacket and a pair of jeans. Gosh, he looked so dashing. So successful and artistic. I nearly fell to the floor when I saw him. We hugged and then spent the next hours talking ourselves silly. I felt like I hadn't said so many words to anyone in my life. When he asked about Kenny, I told him the truth— that I wasn't happy in my marriage and that I'd made a mistake. And after that, he placed his hand over mine on the table, looked me in the eyes, and asked me to come up to his hotel with him. Nothing in my mind or body told me not to go. I realized that I'd actually agreed to meet him that night just for this."

Aria was breathless. It was hard to imagine her mother and Judah together, so many years before Aria hung around his office, watching the world roll by from his window.

"I guess you know what I'm going to tell you next," Bethany said.

Aria shook her head at first, unsure. A few ideas came to her: that Kenny had found out about the affair and forbade Bethany to ever see him again or that Judah had abandoned her after their one night together to return to his career.

But then, the realization struck Aria so hard that she nearly fell off the bed.

"No," she breathed.

Bethany nodded, her eyes filling with tears.

"Judah? Really?" Aria gaped at her mother, unsure what to say. She felt as though her heart had exploded, as though every conceivable thing she'd once known about the world had been wrong.

"I didn't tell him until many years after you were born," Bethany whispered. "Because Kenny had made me sign a prenup, and I had no idea how I could care for myself or my children on my own. I had never really worked before, and I was terrified. Gosh, I hate how much fear has dictated my life."

Aria burned with a mix of horror and intrigue. *All this time, Kenny hadn't been her father? All this time, she'd been with her father, an architect genius, at Savannah College of Art and Design.*

"I knew you were going to meet Judah when you went to college," Bethany went on. "And when you started your first semester, I expected to hear from him. But I didn't! In fact, I didn't know how chummy you two were until that Christmas when you spoke about your brilliant Professor Heskew."

"Why didn't you tell me then?" Aria asked.

"At that point, I figured your life was out of my hands," Bethany breathed. "But I regret it. Not too many years after that, you grew to hate Kenny so much that you abandoned Savannah and you abandoned your family. And now, you're here and on your own."

This was the first time Bethany had referred to Aria's apartment.

"But Judah is worried about you," Bethany continued

very quietly. "He said you'd come to Savannah and that you'd maybe figured some stuff out. He wants you to go back to school, honey. He believes in your talent so much. He says..." Bethany paused, searching for the right words. "He says you're a combination of his talents and mine, with your unique spin. After he said that, I couldn't stop crying. It felt wonderful to be remembered for a talent I'd once thought I had."

It had gotten late. Outside, fireworks began to explode in the night sky over Martha's Vineyard, and, through the open windows, you could hear the raucous Vineyard revelers, all celebrating summer and all the magic it had brought.

"Can you stay tonight?" Aria asked her mother.

Bethany's eyes brightened, but her expression was both pained and shocked. She clearly hadn't expected Aria to be open to her story and accepting of her past.

"I can stay," Bethany said softly.

And at that moment, Aria wanted to burrow her face against her mother's shoulder and tell her how much she loved her and wished Bethany had shown this side of herself throughout her childhood.

It was a revelation to learn that Aria and her mother were more alike than she'd thought. But more than that, Aria now knew that Kenny Baldwin was not her father. Judah Heskew was. She wasn't sure what to do with that information. Not yet.

Chapter Twenty

As Bethany slept in Aria's bed that night, Aria stood quietly at the counter, her mind whirring. The fireworks had quit, and a strange quiet had settled over the island. What her mother had just told her had completely torn her apart. But with a funny jump, she reached for her phone, remembering yet another thing that had happened in the past few hours: She'd told Cole that she was in love with him.

Cole had texted back just one thing.

COLE: I love you, too.

Aria's heart shattered. Exhilarated and overwhelmed, she raced for the door and stepped into the heat of the July night, her eyes to the stars. It seemed impossible that she could be this happy, and it seemed impossible that such goodness could exist.

The next morning, Aria and Bethany showered, dressed, and grabbed a coffee from a downtown Edgartown coffee shop. Afterward, Aria drove them out to

Carmella's seaside cottage. When Aria had described the old place to Bethany, she'd been intrigued and asked to see it. "Maybe I can help you decide how to refurbish it. If you don't mind my input." Aria was thrilled.

At the cottage, Aria watched as her mother paced through the living room, the bedroom, the kitchen, and the exterior porch. Her eyes spun thoughtfully. Occasionally, she reached out to knock her fist against a piece of wood or a cabinet, then muttered to herself. It was difficult for Aria to remember that Bethany hadn't dealt with architecture at all for decades. With every movement she made, she seemed more like a natural.

"We need to hire some contractors," Bethany said out on the porch, her voice resolute. "Does your friend Carmella have someone she trusts?"

"I can ask," Aria said, watching as her mother typed notes to herself on her phone about the future of the seaside cottage. Just peering over her shoulder, Aria realized her mother's ideas were more specific than hers. "I can't believe you haven't done this in years."

Bethany nodded her head exactly once, then slid her phone into her purse. "I'm starving," she announced. "Are you?"

Aria took her mother to the sailing bar where she normally worked, where they ordered BLTs and French fries and chatted easily.

"I worked at a place sort of like this in Savannah," Bethany said. "It was hard to make ends meet and do my coursework, but I managed it. Judah used to come in all the time and bother me." She laughed, then took a bite of BLT. This was the first time in years that Aria had seen her mother eat carbs.

As they finished their lunch, Cole walked through the

door, tanned and smiling. Aria had written him briefly to say that her mother had made a spontaneous visit that ultimately changed her life forever. Cole was intrigued.

Bethany's eyes widened as Cole approached. He was the young man who'd been on the sailboat with them last autumn— the young man Kenny had detested and forbade Aria from speaking to. She stood, shook Cole's hand, and said, "Aria tells me you've been a big help to her this year."

"It was nothing," Cole said.

"It was everything," Bethany assured him, gesturing for Cole to sit at their table. As they dropped into their chairs, she leaned across the table and said, "I don't know how to tell you this, Cole. But I've made a number of mistakes in my life— and Aria seems to have been able to see all the way through them."

"I don't know about that," Aria said.

Bethany winced as Cole shifted his gaze from Aria back to Bethany. Aria's cheeks burned with embarrassment. This was the first time she and Cole had seen one another since the "I love you" incident. Under the table, he placed his hand on her thigh, and she took it. She thought she might faint.

"Aria and I are together," Cole said simply. "She's the best thing that's happened to me in years. I hope I've offered her at least a little bit of support during this confusing time."

Bethany's face brightened. After a long pause, she said, "Aria, I knew you weren't happy with Ben."

Aria murmured. "Mom..."

"Let me say this," Bethany continued. "When I saw you and Ben together, I remembered how I felt when I married Kenny. I knew marrying him was a good thing for my bank account and security, but I felt my creativity drying up as I walked down the aisle. I felt my soul curling up and dying. I always knew you were strong, Aria. But the fact that you've gone after what you want shows me just how strong you are." Bethany swallowed, then pushed it one step further. "And I know you'll go back to school eventually to get your degree when the time is right."

Aria's cheeks were flushed. Her mother had hardly complimented her in her life, and now, it was like the compliments were flowing freely, as wild as a raging river.

"I'll consider going back to school," Aria said softly, "if you consider leaving Kenny."

Bethany's lips parted with surprise. After a dramatic pause, during which Aria was sure she would scream at Aria for saying something so heinous, Bethany dropped her head back and burst with laughter. Aria and Cole exchanged worried smiles. This was certainly the weirdest day of Aria's life.

"Why don't we have a drink?" Bethany brightened and turned toward the current bartender, ordering a beer for herself. Aria and Cole opted for a beer, as well, as Aria's head spun. Her mother had certainly never drunk anything except white wine. Who was this woman?

When the bartender arrived with their beers, Bethany raised hers so that it glinted in the July sunshine. "The thing is, darling," Bethany began, "I already left him."

As Bethany closed her eyes and began to drink, Aria's jaw dropped. "Mom? What!" She felt both giddy and insane. Cole's grip around her hand intensified. He knew she needed support.

"So, if that's all you needed to consider returning to school, it's been done," Bethany continued.

"Why? How?" Aria had a million questions, but none of them seemed quite right.

"After Judah called me, I couldn't stop thinking about you and about my life and about all the secrets I've kept from both my children and myself," Bethany said, her smile loose. "So, a few nights ago, after your father got back from some golf outing, I walked up to him with two suitcases packed and said, 'Kenny, I'm leaving you.' He laughed in my face and told me I never would, not really. And that's when I walked out the door."

Aria was flabbergasted. *How had her mother turned her back on all that money? Hadn't she worshiped it for years?*

"I'm sure I'll find new ways to regret this decision, too," Bethany continued. "But once I started driving northeast to you, Aria, I felt a freedom that I had forgotten was possible. Naturally, your father has already canceled all my credit cards, and I'll need to speak with a lawyer immediately. But..." She trailed off, then added, "But I'm finally doing something for me. Something that doesn't have anything to do with money. And I know, somehow, I'll be fine."

Aria was shocked. As she stirred with worry, Cole managed to say, "If you need a place to stay, my family has a number of guest rooms. It would be no problem."

"That's so kind of you, Cole," Bethany said. "Aria and I are supposed to meet with a contractor tomorrow to discuss the next steps on the seaside cottage. Maybe I'll stick around to see that project through."

"I'd love your help," Aria breathed.

"Then it's settled," Bethany said, her voice wavering, as though nothing was that settled.

* * *

The next evening, Aria and Bethany were invited to the Remington House for dinner. They'd spent the better part of the afternoon with a contractor, discussing the intricacies of the work required at the cottage, and Carmella had been so smitten with their understanding of the beauty of the old place that she'd insisted they make a beautiful meal for them.

"We have a big family," Carmella said as they walked out of the sea cottage, her hand wrapped gently around Georgia's head as she slept on her chest. "We're always eager to get together and have dinner. Besides, your daughter has been part of the family for a while now."

"How's that?" Bethany asked.

"She babysits Georgia for me," Carmella explained. "Even during the months when Georgia took a real liking to crying, Aria was there to calm her down. I secretly called her the baby whisperer."

Aria laughed, watching her mother's expression, which beamed with confusion and joy. And at that moment, Aria found herself imagining her mother as a grandmother to Aria's children, holding them as they cried or slept.

This was perhaps the first time Aria had acknowledged to herself that she did want to grow up— if only a little bit.

"What a beautiful home," Bethany said as they turned into the driveway in front of the Remington House. A moment later, Cole popped out of the front door, waving. "That boy is smitten," Bethany joked.

On the back porch, Alyssa and Maggie had set the table as Nancy finished up the cooking in the kitchen, shooing everyone out of her way as she went. Now that it was July, Alyssa was about five months pregnant, and Maggie was just a couple of months behind her. When they explained the story of their pregnancies to Bethany, Bethany chuckled and said, "This family is only getting bigger. How exciting!"

"That's not all," Carmella said toward the end of the table, her cheeks burning pink.

Elsa turned to gape at her sister. "What do you mean? Carmella? Do you have a secret?"

Carmella's smile illuminated her face. "When I started reading my mother's old diaries, I realized that being a mother was the single greatest gift I've ever had. And that Cody was a perfect father and partner. Why wouldn't I want to do it again before it's too late?"

"So, you're trying?" Maggie asked, her voice high-pitched.

Carmella placed her hand on her lower stomach. "It didn't take long."

"Carmella!" Elsa rushed forward and wrapped her arms around her sister. Together, they held one another as tears rained down their cheeks.

Aria remembered that recently, Elsa hadn't known how to take the news of the seaside cottage and their mother's affair. It seemed Carmella and Elsa found a way through that storm, thankfully.

"I feel like I came to this island at a very interesting time," Bethany said contemplatively.

"You did," Carmella assured her. "But what brought you here? And will you be staying long?"

"I left my husband," Bethany said, her voice resolute. "Aria and I are going to put the cottage back together again. And after that? I don't know what I'll do. But I'm sort of excited about that."

"As you should be," Carmella breathed.

"You're very brave," Elsa said. "Starting over is one of the hardest things in the world. But it's often worth it if you're willing to make the leap."

Everyone was silent for a moment, soaking in Elsa's words.

"You know, Aria," Carmella began, her voice quiet. "I don't have any need for that cottage. But I'd like to keep it in the family." Her eyes turned from Cole back to Aria and then to Cole again.

Cole and Aria looked at one another, and in this moment of silence, Aria felt as though she could see many, many years into their future— years of love and hardship and babies and jobs, years of frigid winters and gorgeous summers and long afternoons of sailing.

Cole placed his hand on Aria's lower back and tugged her closer to him, laughing. "I don't think we can turn an offer like that down, Aria. Do you?"

Chapter Twenty-One

This time, Aria returned to Savannah by car.

She sat in her mother's passenger seat with a pair of sunglasses on, her blond hair whipping in the wind as she and her mother discussed architecture, art, poetry, and anything else that came to their minds. Bethany was well versed in just about everything, it seemed like, and now that she'd spent so many years with all this information inside of her, it spilled out all at once.

"Where have you been keeping all of this?" Aria asked outside of a gas station in Virginia, her eyes alight.

Bethany shrugged as she filled the car with gas. She was tanner than Aria had seen her in years, and her hair was tinged with blonde and gray. "Never underestimate any woman, Aria. We've all done what we can to survive this long."

It was late July. Bethany had spent the last three weeks in Martha's Vineyard, overseeing the work at the sea cottage as the contractors had put it back together again. And already, it was nearly complete, nearly ready for Aria and Cole's big move. Cole had already talked about bringing his sailboat to the dock outside the house, one they'd had rebuilt to ensure its stability. Aria could just picture herself and Cole there in the future, waking up in one another's arms, prepared to sail out right from their dock.

During July, Bethany had gotten very cozy with Elsa, Carmella, Janine, and Nancy. Although Elsa and Carmella no longer lived in the Remington House, they were always just a phone call away and often swept through during evenings to say hello and have a glass of wine or lemonade on the back porch. In this way, Bethany had begun to heal from her past trauma. She'd begun to speak about how Kenny had actually treated her all this time, and Carmella, Elsa, Nancy, and Janine had helped her to understand just how not normal it had been. It turned out that Janine, too, had been married to a very manipulative man who'd cheated on her with her best friend. "Year after year, it just seemed more normal," Janine had explained of Jack's behavior. "I was pretty sure that was how all husbands treated their wives." It was even more miraculous to learn that Janine and her best friend, Maxine, were friendly now that the ex-husband had died. "Life is the strangest thing I've ever known," Bethany joked of this.

With Bethany frequently off with the Remington family, Cole and Aria had been left to enjoy as many evenings as they could. Their eight months of tiptoeing around their feelings for one another had made them fiery with passion, and they found themselves saying all the things they'd never said, unwilling to leave a single thing out. Cole confessed that he'd fallen for her the minute he'd seen her on that sailboat in the Caribbean, and Aria said, "I knew you felt something, too!" And they laughed about this, then kissed some more, as though they were teenagers who'd just discovered the concept of love.

Aria had announced that she wanted to finish her degree, hoping to take online classes, and she was prepared to contact her advisor about the situation. To this, Bethany had said, "No. We're going. They want to see you and know that you're serious this time. They want to be sure that you're worth it."

Aria had a hunch that Bethany's insistence on going to Savannah in the first place had almost everything to do with seeing Professor Judah Heskew again.

Because everything had been so busy since Bethany's arrival, Aria hadn't gotten up the nerve to contact Judah about her discovery that, all this time, he'd been her father. Now that they were on the road, only hours away from Savannah, a city that both she and her mother adored, the expectation for the reunion ahead filled Aria with a mix of awe and fear.

"You know," Aria began thoughtfully, "some of the other students said that I was Judah's favorite and that I had no talent but was treated well anyway."

To this, Bethany turned to glare at Aria, her hands still at ten-and-two. "That's ridiculous."

Aria didn't go on to say that that had been part of the reason she'd dropped out of college in the first place, that she hadn't liked feeling like her skills weren't worthy.

"I mean, you don't know, "Aria pointed out. "I never showed you any of my blueprints."

Bethany's lips twisted as she returned her gaze to the road. "Judah sent some of them over."

Aria's heart banged away in her chest. "You're kidding. When?"

"This week," Bethany said.

Aria's jaw dropped. "You've been talking."

Bethany shrugged.

"You told him you're leaving, Dad."

"I haven't told him yet."

"But you're going to," Aria breathed.

"It's a fact of my life," Bethany said. "I suppose it would be weird to leave it out."

"What about Judah's wife?" Aria asked, side-eyeing her mother.

Bethany had no answer to that. Apparently, she and Judah's conversations hadn't gone deep enough for her to know what awaited her, romance-wise, in Savannah. Aria's apprehension grew.

"In any case, your blueprints were stellar, Aria," Bethany said sternly. "Judah and I had a fifteen-email exchange regarding your talents. But beyond that, I've seen you at work on the cottage the past few weeks. You already have instincts that it takes some architects years to hone."

Aria folded her lips, trying not to smile too wide. She'd never imagined her mother giving her such a specific compliment before.

"Have you talked to Natalie or Gregory yet?" Aria asked. "About leaving Dad, I mean."

"I spoke to Natalie on the phone a few days ago," Bethany said. "It'll come as a surprise to you that Natalie supports me. I think it's just a matter of good timing, though."

"Why's that?"

"Natalie moved out of her home with Malcolm," Bethany said. "She can't take his arrogance another second."

"Wow. And what about Gregory?"

"Gregory has made it clear he's not ready to talk to me," Bethany said, her voice wavering.

"Maybe he just needs time."

"Or maybe he's just another man who can't possibly understand how stifling it can be as a woman sometimes," Bethany said quietly. "I tried to raise my children as best as I could, with compassion. But with Gregory, your father was always his greatest idol, and I suppose I can't change that."

When Bethany parked the car on the outskirts of Savannah College of Art and Design, Bethany and Aria sat, wordless, in the front seat of the car for a full minute. It was terribly hot and humid, reminiscent of that long-ago day— nearly a year ago— when Aria had sat in Judah's office and eaten ice cream sandwiches. That had been the day she'd first learned the other students had no respect for her. That had been the beginning of the end.

Then again, had she never dropped out of college, she never would have fallen in love with Cole, and she never would have met Carmella. And she never would have been back at Savannah College, diving into the past with her mother by her side.

Everything happened for a reason. She had to believe that.

Bethany and Aria walked slowly through campus. Throughout, only a few students walked past them, all of them slow from the heat. As there was no breeze, the moss on the huge trees hung limply.

"I used to live there." Bethany stopped in front of one of the old dorms, her eyes shimmering with memories. "I lived there with a girl named Surrey. She came from Mississippi. I wonder what happened to her. And gosh. I still remember when Judah met me in front of this very dorm so we could grab food together, go for a walk, or find somewhere to make out."

"Mom!" Aria cackled.

Bethany's smile was youthful, reminiscent of those long-ago days that she could never get back. "We were happy as clams," Bethany said as she turned to continue their walk toward the architecture building. "I don't think we ever could have imagined what the future would bring. But there was always this sense, back then, that whatever came next would be better than what we already had. I suppose you have to grow up to learn that's not always true."

When they reached the architecture building, Aria and her mother greeted Aria's advisor and sat with him for a full hour, going over Aria's previous class credits and creating a plan so that Aria could graduate via online classes.

"I see no reason you can't graduate by next spring," the advisor said, adjusting his glasses on his nose. "Most every degree can be secured online these days. And if you're sure you don't want to be in Savannah any longer, we can accommodate you."

Aria's mind flashed with images of her beautiful three years on campus, where she'd been very lonely yet focused on her career.

"I have a home on Martha's Vineyard," Aria explained. "I'm needed back there."

The advisor signed Aria up for six online classes for the next semester, which was a doozy of a schedule, then shook Aria and Bethany's hands before heading out. When they stepped into the foyer, Bethany's legs quivered so much that her knees nearly knocked together.

"He said he'd meet us downstairs," Bethany said, her eyes scanning the stairs.

Aria wondered what this was like, seeing someone you'd loved for the first time in twenty-five years. She imagined it was terrifying, filled with questions and fears. Bethany tapped her hair gently, as though any last touch-ups could fix what the humidity had done to it.

"You look beautiful, Mom," Aria told her, because she did. There was a light in Bethany's eyes that Aria had never seen before. There was an expectation for a better life.

Suddenly, Professor Judah Heskew appeared on the steps. His hair was wild and curly, and his glasses were thick, and as he smiled down upon them— a woman he'd loved and the daughter they'd made together— his eyes filled with tears.

Aria had never seen Professor Heskew cry before. Always, she'd seen him as a powerful and intellectual man who wasn't prone to emotions.

But now, he wasn't Professor Heskew anymore. He was her father.

Judah reached the bottom of the stairs and stood in front of Bethany and Aria for a couple of wordless seconds before opening his arms. Bethany hurried into them, letting out a single sob. Aria felt her stomach flip over at the sight of them. *This couldn't be happening. Could it?*

When their hug broke, both Judah and Bethany's cheeks glinted with tears. After a very long and ponderous silence, Judah said, "Why don't we get something to eat?"

Aria couldn't imagine eating at a time like this, but it seemed like the only thing to do.

Together, the three of them stepped into the thick heat of the early evening, then headed toward their hotel, which was located on the other side of Forsyth House, near the Mercer-Williams House Museum. There, Aria stood at the counter with her mother as Bethany checked them in, collected their room keys, then led them to the hotel restaurant, which was said to have a wonderful chef. It was only five-thirty, but Aria and Bethany had been too nervous to eat lunch. Judah confessed that he, too, hadn't eaten all day. He was starving.

Judah suggested they order an appetizer and a round of drinks, which Bethany jumped at the chance for. Aria knew she wanted to calm her nerves. Together, they ordered a bottle of wine from a region Judah recommended, as Bethany made the first mention of their past.

"I remember you went to Italy that year after we graduated. I was so jealous."

Judah's eyes glinted with the memory. "I invited you to come to visit me."

"I didn't have the money for that," Bethany reminded him, not unkindly. "But it would have been a dream. I imagine you found someone else to make your time worthwhile. An Italian woman, maybe."

"I was too broken-hearted about losing you to even glance at another woman," Judah said softly.

Aria had the sudden sensation that she wasn't there at all, that she was watching the dinner unfold from the ceiling above.

When the waiter arrived, he poured them each a glass of wine, and Judah raised his as he said, "I don't know why it took us this long." Aria and Bethany locked eyes before they drank. The air was taut with tension.

"Excuse me," Bethany said suddenly, rising to her

feet. "I'll be right back." She fled down the hallway and disappeared into a bathroom. Aria watched her go, then turned her head to find Judah in front of her, giving her that same mysterious smile that she knew so well from her years at the university.

Suddenly, with just the two of them there, Aria was no longer frightened.

"Why didn't you ever tell me?" she blurted.

Judah's laughter was big and brassy. "I don't know. I suppose I didn't want to hurt Bethany. From what you told me, it sounded like she was happy in her life. That she'd become this Texas socialite, the perfect wife of a very rich man. You couldn't have been more incorrect."

Aria nodded. "I admit I was wrong about my mother. I've been wrong about so many things."

"Welcome to adulthood," Judah said.

Aria held the silence for a moment, rolling a sip of wine around her tongue. "What did you think when you first saw me?"

Judah's face looked pained. "I wasn't sure at first if it really was you."

"But you knew that my mother had your child?"

"Of course," Judah said. "She let me know about you when you were born. And she also made it clear she wasn't leaving Kenny. By then, I'd met my wife, and I just assumed..." He shook his head, at a loss. "I don't know. That she was right, I suppose. But I couldn't imagine why she would allow you to come to the Savannah College of Art and Design, not when she knew I was a professor here."

"It wasn't her idea," Aria said. "And I didn't want her to have anything to do with it."

"She told me," Judah said.

Aria's heart ballooned. She sipped her wine again, her thoughts swirling. "What about your wife?" she rasped.

Judah raised his shoulders. "We've been in the middle of a messy divorce for over a year."

"You never said anything." Aria remembered last September, asking Judah about marriage, about if it was worth it. At the time, she'd needed to break up with Ben, but she hadn't known how.

"I didn't want to complain about my divorce to the daughter who didn't even know I was her father. All I wanted to do was help you hone your architectural talents. And maybe remind you that someone on this campus cared for you, even when you were convinced you were alone."

The sentiment was one of the kindest Aria had ever heard.

"I just can't figure out one thing," Aria said, her eyes to the hallway, watching for her mother. "Who sent me the newspaper clipping?"

Judah's cheeks were red with embarrassment. "That would be my ex-wife."

Aria's jaw dropped. "You're kidding."

"I wish I was. She knew about you, about how I felt about being able to get to know you here on campus, and I think she was overwhelmed with jealousy. She wanted to destroy my reputation by sending the newspaper clipping to you, but I guess it backfired."

"How did you figure out she'd mailed the clipping to me?"

"I got a bill for a private detective who'd hunted down your exact address." Judah sighed.

Aria's laughter sounded strange. "It *was* a messy divorce."

"Yes."

"But it's sort of ironic, isn't it? Without that news-paper clipping, maybe my mother would never have left Kenny, and maybe I never would have returned to school."

Judah's smile widened. "You're coming back. You're going to graduate."

"I have to," Aria said. "Architecture is the only thing that ever made sense to me."

"I remember saying the exact same thing when I was your age," Judah said softly. "Around the time that your mother and I broke up, and I felt that nothing in life would ever make sense— I knew that I would always have architecture."

Chapter Twenty-Two

That night with Aria's mother and father was one she would remember for the rest of her life. Together, they ate decadently, shared stories, and found new ways to laugh. It felt like medicine against the horrors of the past. Although Aria had no idea what would happen next or whether Judah and Bethany would ever find love with one another again, she knew they'd all taken tremendous steps forward as people. Maybe that was all that mattered.

Upstairs in the hotel room, Aria washed her face, got into bed, and called Cole on the phone to tell him what had happened.

"My mom looks totally smitten," she said. "Like a teenage girl or something."

"This is such a wild story," Cole said.

"Where are you tonight?" Aria asked.

"I'm at the cottage, actually," Cole explained with a laugh. "Since the bedroom is ready to go, I thought I'd move my bed and mattress in. The place is a million times better than either of our apartments. I figure we had better just move in when you get back."

Aria pictured Cole seated at the edge of the bed they would share in their first home together; she pictured him year after year in that cottage, out on the back porch, watching the waves lap up against the dock, and the sunlight play across the water. She pictured herself at the kitchen table, drawing up blueprints for whatever architecture project she was in the midst of. She imagined the kind of life she could be proud of.

Nearly three hours later, Bethany returned to the bedroom, her eyes shining from too many glasses of wine. She collapsed in bed next to Aria and stared at the ceiling, her hands stretched across her stomach.

"You look smitten," Aria teased.

Bethany rolled over and propped up her head with her elbow. "I felt like I was twenty-one again," she said quietly.

"That sounds like magic."

"It really was," Bethany breathed.

"What are you going to do?" Aria asked.

"I don't know," Bethany said honestly. "But I can't go that many decades without seeing him again." Bethany gazed at her daughter thoughtfully, then added, "How did you get so smart, Aria?"

"What are you talking about?"

"I just mean, how did you know to follow your heart at such a young age? Why did it take me nearly fifty years to figure out what you figured out at twenty-four?"

"Mom, I haven't figured anything out," Aria assured her. Yet even as she said it, images of Cole and the sea cottage flashed through her mind, and she smiled and cuddled up next to her mother.

Very quietly, her mother added, "Getting to know you better the past few weeks has been the greatest gift of my life, you know."

Aria could hardly breathe. Blinking back tears, she whispered, "I can't believe I went twenty-four years not knowing you at all."

* * *

Aria and Bethany remained in Savannah, getting to know Judah in a brand-new way for the next few days. They walked Savannah, ate at fancy restaurants, laughed uproariously, and eventually abandoned their hotel to stay at Judah's beautiful home, which had been built in the 1800s and was filled with character and "Savannah ghosts."

Aria felt as though she was allowed a front-row seat to watch her parents fall back in love again. Never had she seen her mother laugh so deliciously. Never had she witnessed such an easy conversation. Never had she eaten so well.

When Cole announced that he planned to sail back down to Savannah to pick Aria up, Aria urged him not to. "It's okay! It's too far, and I can just drive back or take the bus." But Cole said he was only a couple of hours away. "You can either come with me or not, but I couldn't wait to see you."

Aria's heart doubled in size. When she announced Cole's arrival to Judah and Bethany, they decided to come with her to the docks to see her off. Judah even carried her suitcase, looking proud and happy and strong in ways Aria had always wished Kenny was.

Cole's sailboat appeared on the horizon, surging

toward them with the immensity of the Atlantic Ocean behind it. Cole was on the edge of the boat, his strong arms drawing himself through the heavy southern winds and the pummeling waves. On the dock, Aria took a deep breath, sizzling with expectation for the trip back. It would be nights filled with moonlight, stars sparkling in the sky above, and Cole's strong arms around her, guiding her home.

Coming next in the Katama Bay Series

Pre – Order Summer Rush

Other Books by Katie

The Vineyard Sunset Series

Sisters of Edgartown Series

Secrets of Mackinac Island Series

A Katama Bay Series

A Mount Desert Island Series

A Nantucket Sunset Series

Connect with Katie Winters

BookBub
Facebook
Newsletter